DAMNATION
SPAWN
AF378306

SPAWN®: DAMNATION
ISBN 1 84023 030 4

Published by Titan Books Ltd
42 - 44 Dolben St
London SE1 0UP
In association with Image Comics™

Spawn®, its logo and its symbol are registered trademarks ™ 1996 of Todd
McFarlane Productions, Inc. All other related characters are Trademark ™ and
Copyright © Todd McFarlane Productions, Inc. Copyright © 1996 Todd
McFarlane Productions, Inc. All Rights Reserved.
No portion of this book may be reproduced or transmitted in any form or by
any means, without the express, written, permission of the publisher. Names,
characters, places and incidents featured in this publication are either the
product of the author's imagination or used fictitiously. Any resemblance to
actual persons (living or dead) is entirely coincidental.

This book collects issues 49 – 53 of the Image Comics' series *Spawn*.

British Library Cataloguing-In-Publication data. A catalogue record for this
book is available from the British Library.

First edition: March 1999
10 9 8 7 6 5 4 3 2 1

Printed in Italy.

Other *Spawn* titles now available from Titan Books:

Spawn: Creation
Spawn: Evolution
Spawn: Revelation
Spawn: Escalation
Spawn: Confrontation
Spawn: Retribution
Spawn: Transformation
Spawn: Abduction
Spawn: Sanction
Spawn: Angela

Spawn: The Making of the Movie

DAMNATION

SPAWN

TODD McFARLANE
with GREG CAPULLO and DANNY MIKI

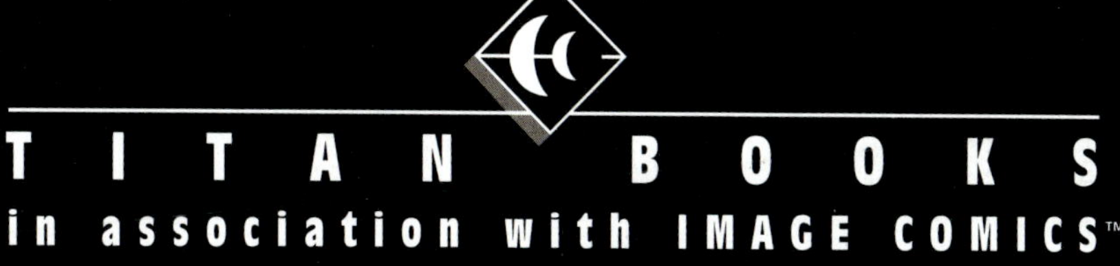

Hell. It exists. Believe it.

Al Simmons does, and so he should. He's been there. Of course, he doesn't remember much about the experience, he was too busy dying in agonising pain, having been betrayed and murdered by men he trusted, men he even called friends. That sort of thing can throw you a curve, trust me. Spent five years there... at least as you lot measure time.

But unlike most of the poor saps that take that final, irrevocable nose-dive into the abyss, Al Simmons had a return ticket. He came back.

Though not as Al Simmons, oh no. If you make it out of there you can be damn sure there's a price tag involved, and it's pinned right on your immortal soul.

In Al's case, his Achilles heel was his wife, Wanda. Loved her so much that when demon lord Malebolgia offered him the means to see Wanda again he jumped at the chance.

Of course, he was set up. Transformed into a Hellspawn, a necroplasmically empowered general in the army of the damned, Al's new look came complete with living body armour and cape, not to mention extra-crispy deep fried flesh.

He'd been dealt a hand from a diabolically stacked deck, see. Sure, he

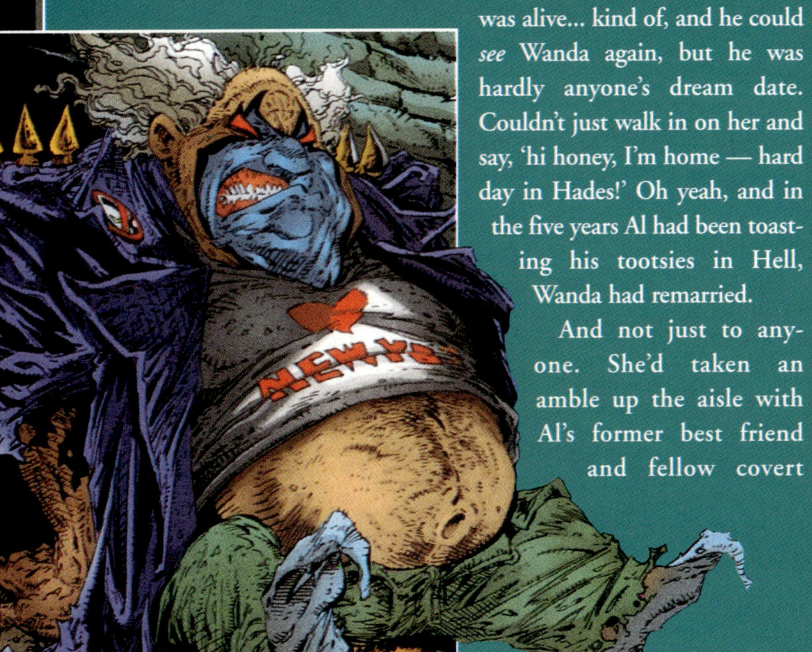

was alive... kind of, and he could *see* Wanda again, but he was hardly anyone's dream date. Couldn't just walk in on her and say, 'hi honey, I'm home — hard day in Hades!' Oh yeah, and in the five years Al had been toasting his tootsies in Hell, Wanda had remarried.

And not just to anyone. She'd taken an amble up the aisle with Al's former best friend and fellow covert government agent Terry Fitzgerald, a guy who Spawn figures may have even had a hand in his death... but hey, I'm getting ahead of myself. There's a whole lot more pain and torment to fill you in on before all that.

Did I mention Wanda and Terry had a kid? Well, anyway, a kid was what Wanda wanted above all else, and the one thing Al couldn't give her. A real double-whammy to start off the old afterlife.

From there? Downhill all the way, I'm not sorry to say. Since

his creation, he's been dogged by warrior angels looking to bag his head for their wall, tormented by religious nuts with dissection on their minds, harassed by mobsters and cyborg killing-machines, hunted by the cops, hounded by his ex-boss Jason Wynn — one of the few humans with any real promise, it has to be said — and generally used as a whipping boy by any half-assed maniac with a grudge.

Even his costume hates him. The thing's got a mind of its own these days, wants to be its own symbiote or something like that. But then that's the trouble with K-Models, no respect for their elders.

Friends? Well, there's old

man Cogliostro, who fancies himself as Spawn's mentor, but he's been warned off, told to 'fess up all he knows or pick another hard luck case. Even the bums Spawn shares an alley with, they're beginning to wonder about Al's loyalty. Rejected by the rejected. How low can you go?

But best of all is Terry. Now this guy was Al's blood brother, they trusted each other with their lives. But Spawn, he finds out that Terry's protecting Jason Wynn, even though he's actually working from the inside out, trying to get evidence that'll nail Wynn once and for all. Now Spawn, he puts two and two together, and comes up with conspiracy. Terry works for Wynn, Wynn had him killed — or so he thinks — therefore Terry is the enemy. Don't ya just love it?

And me? Well, I suppose I haven't helped things. In fact, if you were being really harsh, you'd have to say I've, well, stirred the cauldron a bit, put the dead cat among the vultures, *clowned* around. See, Spawny, he doesn't appreciate the honour of lead- ing Hell's army, doesn't get that there's some real demons would like to have been chosen by the big 'M'. And, well, to put not too fine a point on it, I'd like to send him back to Hell... for all eternity this time.

If, that is, he doesn't do it himself first!

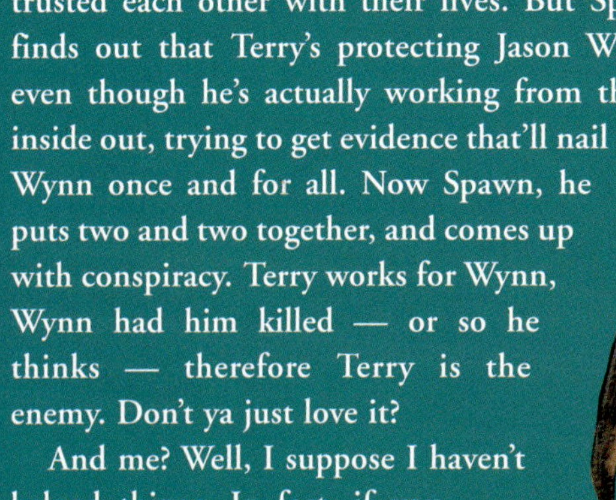

image
SPAWN
49
MAY
$1.95
$2.75 Canada
HELTER SKELTER

KNOCK KNOCK

GRANNIE? MAY I COME IN?

OF COURSE, AL, ANYTIME.

AND YOU DON'T NEED TO KNOCK, YOU'RE ALWAYS WELCOME HERE.

TO TELL YOU THE TRUTH, I'D LIKE IT IF YOU VISITED MORE OFTEN. I HOPE THAT DOESN'T SOUND SELFISH.

NO, IT DOESN'T. I'M SORRY IT'S BEEN SO LONG SINCE MY LAST VISIT. * I'VE BEEN TRYING TO PUT A FEW THINGS IN ORDER... WHICH IS WHY I'M HERE, ACTUALLY.

* ISSUE 38 -- Tom.

SOMETHING IS HAPPENING TO ME. AND I CAN'T SEEM TO DO ANYTHING ABOUT IT. THINGS... THINGS YOU CAN'T EVEN IMAGINE ARE SPINNING OUT OF CONTROL.

AND I CAN'T STOP IT.

NOW YOU LISTEN TO ME, BOY. THE LORD BURDENS ALL OF US WITH OUR OWN PERSONAL CROSSES. SOME WILL SEEM A LITTLE HEAVIER THAN OTHERS, BUT GOD KNOWS HOW MUCH EACH OF US CAN BEAR.

I TOLD YOU BEFORE, AL. HE PICKED YOU TO BE ONE OF HIS ANGELS FOR A REASON. IT'S JUST THAT NONE OF US, NOT EVEN YOU WHO LIVE WITH HIM IN HEAVEN, WILL EVER UNDERSTAND THE MYSTERIES OF HIS WAYS.
OUR PART IS JUST HAVING FAITH. GOD WILL TAKE CARE OF THE REST.
IT'S NOT THAT SIMPLE. AT LEAST NOT NOW. WHAT'S HAPPENING TO ME IS PUTTING OTHERS IN DANGER. INCLUDING YOU.
WHAT'RE YOU SAYING?
I DON'T KNOW IF IT'S SAFE FOR ME TO KEEP VISITING YOU.
NO!
DON'T YOU DARE DO THAT TO ME!
I MAY BE OLD BUT I'M NOT STUPID. I'VE SENSED SOMETHING HAS BEEN GNAWING AWAY AT YOU FOR QUITE SOME TIME. BUT YOU DON'T RUN AWAY FROM THAT.
YOU NEVER RAN WHEN YOU WERE ALIVE, SO DON'T START NOW. THIS FEELING, THIS PREMONITION OF DOOM-- CAST IT ASIDE. DON'T ABANDON THOSE WHO CAN HELP YOU.
WE ALL LOVE YOU TOO MUCH.
I HAVE TO LEAVE. I'M SORRY.
IT'S YOUR INNER DEMONS, ISN'T IT? YOU MUST CONQUER THEM, AL, WITH THE LORD'S HELP, IF YOU EVER WANT TO FIND TRUE PEACE.

N-hnnn...
OPEN WIDE...
Nnnn...
Hmmm...
THAT'S ALL. YOU CAN GET DRESSED NOW.
IT APPEARS THAT EVERYTHING IS IN GOOD WORKING ORDER. I JUST WISH WE DIDN'T HAVE TO DRAG YOU IN HERE EVERY TIME.
BUT JUST TO MAKE SURE, I'M SENDING YOU TO A SPECIALIST. HE'S A DOCTOR WHO DEALS WITH NEUROLOGICAL SYMPTOMS.
WHY?
WHAT'S WRONG WITH ME?

NOTHING, I HOPE... BUT YOUR FAINTING SPELL TELLS ME THAT SOMETHING WENT WRONG.
I JUST LIKE TO BE CERTAIN I HAVEN'T OVERLOOKED ANYTHING.
* LAST ISSUE -- Tom.
OH, NOW DON'T LOOK SO WORRIED.
THE DOCTOR WILL JUST RUN A FEW TESTS, POSSIBLY A C.A.T. SCAN, JUST TO EASE ALL OUR MINDS. I KNOW YOU'VE BEEN UNDER A GREAT DEAL OF PRESSURE LATELY... ON TOP OF THAT NASTY COUGH YOU'VE HAD... BUT US MEDICAL GEEKS LIKE TO KNOW WHY PEOPLE BLACK OUT FOR NO REASON.
IT HAPPENS TO MOST PEOPLE AT LEAST ONCE IN THEIR LIVES. WE JUST NEVER KNOW WHY.
WHAT CAN I SAY? WE'RE A CURIOUS LOT. SO I'LL SCHEDULE AN APPOINTMENT...?
UH... YEAH, SURE. IF YOU THINK IT'S BEST.
COFF
COFF
COFF
OUT IN THE PARKING LOT, TERRY'S CHEST BEGINS TO TIGHTEN AS HIS MIND SWIRLS WITH FABRICATED IMAGES AND THOUGHTS.
IT TRIGGERS A SLIGHT COUGHING FIT.
HE CURSES HIMSELF FOR NOT DOING SOMETHING EARLIER.

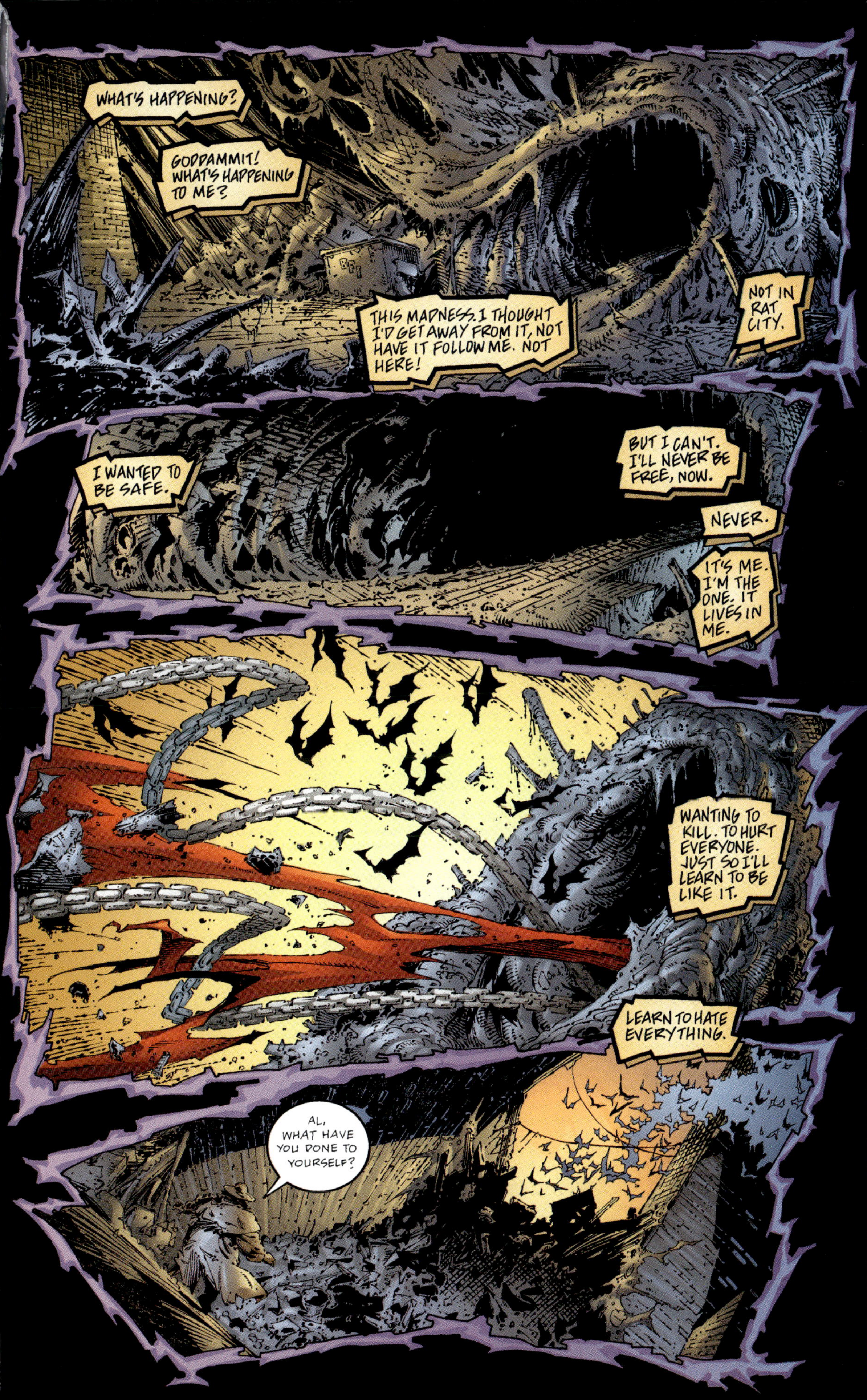

WHAT'S HAPPENING?
GODDAMMIT! WHAT'S HAPPENING TO ME?
THIS MADNESS. I THOUGHT I'D GET AWAY FROM IT, NOT HAVE IT FOLLOW ME. NOT HERE!
NOT IN RAT CITY.
I WANTED TO BE SAFE.
BUT I CAN'T. I'LL NEVER BE FREE, NOW.
NEVER.
IT'S ME. I'M THE ONE. IT LIVES IN ME.
WANTING TO KILL. TO HURT EVERYONE. JUST SO I'LL LEARN TO BE LIKE IT.
LEARN TO HATE EVERYTHING.
AL, WHAT HAVE YOU DONE TO YOURSELF?

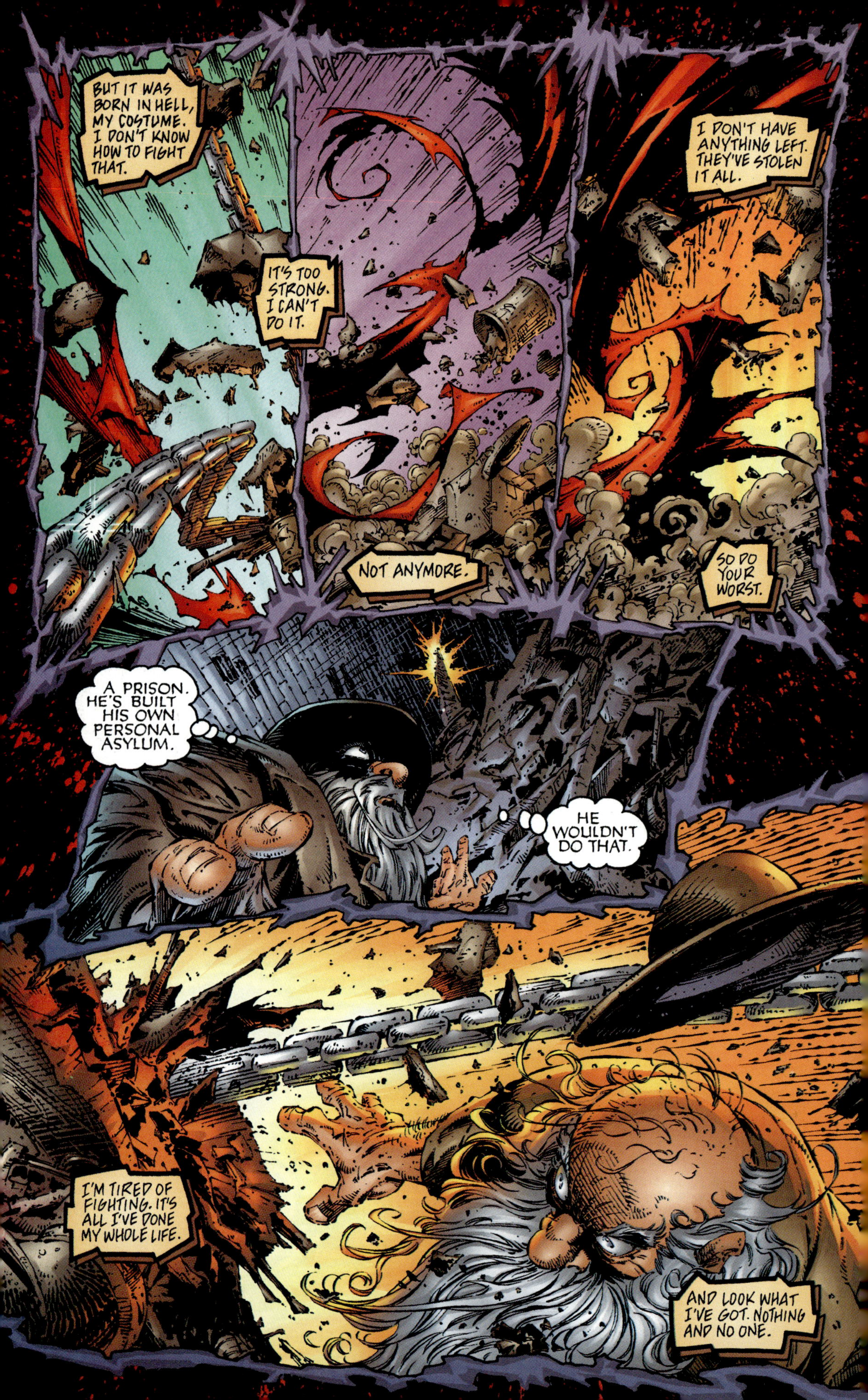

BUT IT WAS BORN IN HELL, MY COSTUME. I DON'T KNOW HOW TO FIGHT THAT.
IT'S TOO STRONG. I CAN'T DO IT.
I DON'T HAVE ANYTHING LEFT. THEY'VE STOLEN IT ALL.
NOT ANYMORE.
SO DO YOUR WORST.
A PRISON. HE'S BUILT HIS OWN PERSONAL ASYLUM.
HE WOULDN'T DO THAT.
I'M TIRED OF FIGHTING. IT'S ALL I'VE DONE MY WHOLE LIFE.
AND LOOK WHAT I'VE GOT. NOTHING AND NO ONE.

THE COSTUME'S GOT SOME KIND OF INFECTION-- MAKING IT ERRATIC. AL DOESN'T KNOW HOW TO READ THE SYMPTOMS. AND IF HE DOESN'T STOP IT FROM SPREADING, THE SYBIOTE WILL ADVANCE TO NECRO-STATE NINE BEFORE IT'S READY FOR THAT LEVEL.
AL!
HELP ME! WHERE'S THE OPENING?

GOT TO GET IN. DON'T HAVE TIME TO WAIT.

I STILL DON'T KNOW HOW THE OLD MAN GOT IN.
BUT HE DID.

MY GOD, AL...
NO.

IN ANOTHER OF THE CITY'S MILLION SHADOWS...
WHAT A SAP. WHAT A MAROON.
IF JASON WYNN IS THE BEST EXAMPLE OF "DISPICABLE" THESE HUMANS CAN MUSTER...
...THEN I COULD BE KING OF THIS PLANET TOMORROW.
HE'S GOT THE EVILNESS, I'LL GIVE HIM THAT, BUT I'M ABLE TO KNEAD HIM JUST TOO EASILY INTO WHATEVER I WANT.
HERO. SCAPEGOAT. ASSASSIN. POLITICIAN. I'VE MADE HIM PLAY 'EM ALL. HE DOESN'T EVEN RESIST MUCH... UNLIKE YOU, MY DEAR FURRY FRIEND.

AT LEAST YOU PUT UP A FIGHT FOR ...
?
IT TAKES A FULL THIRTY SECONDS FOR THE SIGNAL TO PENETRATE.
YES!
YES. YES. YES.
THIS IS PERFECT! SIMMONS IS GETTING CRAPPED ON BY HIS SYMBIOTE. I ALWAYS DID LOVE THOSE K-MODEL UNITS. THEY'RE ALWAYS SO VOLITILE.
HEE HEE!
I MEAN, I KNEW SOMETHING WAS UP WITH SPAWN AND HIS UNIFORM... BUT THIS?! EVEN I COULDN'T HAVE PREDICTED IT WOULD HAPPEN THIS QUICK!
HEE HEE HOHO!
I'M TELLING YOU, LITTLE FRIEND, THIS COULD SAVE ME A COUPLE MONTHS OF GROUNDWORK. JUST THINK-- NOT HAVING TO FOOL AROUND WITH WYNN. OR FITZGERALD. OR BLAKE.
JUST STRAIGHT TO THE MOTHERLODE! BAM! AND SIMMONS HAS A ONE-WAY TICKET BACK TO HELL.
I CAN TASTE THE VICTORY NOW-- GULP!

GOD.

HE WAS ALL I COULD THINK OF THEN. AS THE COSTUME THRASHED ABOUT, TRYING TO SPILL MY GUTS ON THE GROUND, IT WAS GOD I THOUGHT OF.

WHY WOULD HE CREATE ALL THIS?

WHY WOULD HE WANT TO?

DAMN YOU, MALEBOLGIA.

MY ANGER AT HIM WAS ALL I HAD LEFT: THE ONLY DISTRACTION BIG ENOUGH TO HELP ME FORGET THE PAIN.

EVEN AS THE TUMORS GREW AND MY GUTS SPILLED FORTH, IT WAS ANGER AT HIM THAT POSSESSED ME.
GOD MADE SATAN. SATAN MADE HELL. HELL MADE MALEBOLGIA. MALEBOLGIA MADE THIS COSTUME.
SO IT'S FROM HIM. FROM GOD THAT ALL THIS EVIL COMES.
IT'S HIS FAULT.
SOMEHOW, HE WANTED OR NEEDED THIS.
MY LOGIC MADE NO SENSE. IT DIDN'T MATTER. IT SERVED THE PURPOSE UNTIL ANOTHER DISTRACTION APPEARED.
AL! FIGHT IT! FIGHT THE PAIN!
IT'S FEEDING OFF YOUR EMOTIONS!

COGLIOSTRO.
"THE COUNT," HE CALLS HIMSELF. ALWAYS APPEARS OUT OF NO-WHERE, LIKE SOME FRIGGIN' HOODOO MAN.
HE KNOWS THINGS... STUFF HE SHOULDN'T KNOW THE FIRST THING ABOUT. HOW? WHY?
AND HIS EYES. I'LL NEVER FORGET THEM. THEY GLARE WITH A DEFIANCE LIKE I'VE NEVER SEEN.
AT FIRST, IT DIDN'T SEEM TO MATTER WHEN THE CREATURE REACTED, SWALLOWING THE OLD MAN WHOLE.
EVEN WHEN A HUGE, SERPENTINE PIECE OF THE CLOAK SNARED HIM, HE DIDN'T APPEAR SCARED.
IT WAS MORE LIKE HE WAS WAITING FOR IT. SOMEHOW PREPARED FOR WHAT WAS TO HAPPEN.
THE COUNT NEVER FLINCHED. NOT A GODDAMN MUSCLE.

THE MUTATED CLOAK JUST SAT THERE, FROZEN LIKE A GIANT COBRA. I THOUGHT THAT WAS IT.
I DIDN'T NOTICE THE FIRST CONVULSION, BUT EACH ONE AFTER THAT GREW MORE INTENSELY VIOLENT.
ITS THRASHING BECAME A BLUR BEFORE IT ENDED ITS OWN PAIN BY VOMITING UP WHAT WAS POISONING IT:
THE COUNT.
HE ROLLED AROUND A BIT AFTER THE UNHOLY ABORTION, THEN LET FLY A STREAM OF DIALECT NOT FROM THIS PLANET.
WHAT HAPPENED NEXT I DON'T REMEMBER, EXCEPT THAT IT FELT AS IF A HERD OF ANIMALS WAS BEING STUFFED INSIDE ME.

HE TOLD ME AFTERWARDS I WAS UNCONSCIOUS FOR ONLY A FEW SECONDS.
THAT WAS GOOD, HE SAID.

COME ON, BOY. CAPTURE IT. CONTROL IT. HARNESS ITS POWER.
YOU MUST.
IF ANY OF US ARE GOING TO LIVE THROUGH THIS, YOU HAVE TO LEARN HOW TO CAGE THE DEMONS.
MORE RIDDLES. AS THE PAIN PASSED, MY CONFUSION DIDN'T. BUT IT WASN'T THE TIME FOR QUESTIONS.

THAT COULD WAIT. I NEEDED SOMETHING MORE IMPORTANT.
HELP ME. PLEASE.

I'VE BEEN TRYING, AL. DON'T YOU UNDERSTAND? WHY DO YOU THINK I'M HERE?
BECAUSE OF YOU.
MY APPEARANCE HERE ISN'T AN ACCIDENT. NEITHER IS YOURS.
WE NEED EACH OTHER. SO DO OUR SOULS.

THEY'RE HIDING SOME-THING. I KNOW THEY ARE. I CAN SEE IT IN HIS FACE.
DR. ROLLINS
NEUROLOGIST
SUITE 209

IF I'VE GOT A PROBLEM, WHY DON'T THEY JUST SPIT IT OUT? ALL THIS WAITING IS KILLING ME. I'D RATHER HAVE BAD NEWS THAN NO NEWS.
mmmHmm
TAP TAP TAP

I'VE GOT TO GET OUT OF HERE. THIS IS CRAZY. I'M PERFECTLY FINE.
tic tic tic

THEY SAID THIS HAPPENS TO EVERYONE. SO, I SHOULD JUST GO. THAT'S IT! I'M OUTTA HERE.

WELL, MR. FITZGERALD, YOUR CHART APPEARS TO BE IN ORDER. IT LOOKS LIKE DR. BUSINO JUST WANTS ME TO RUN SOME STANDARD TESTS.
NOTHING TO GET EXCITED ABOUT.
I'M DYING. I'M DYING. I'M DYING.
THAT'D BE FINE. WHATEVER YOU NEED, DOCTOR.

PLEASE, MR. FITZGERALD, IT'S OKAY TO BE A LITTLE ANXIOUS. MOST PATIENTS ARE THE FIRST TIME. COME, LET ME SHOW YOU WHAT WE'LL BE LOOKING FOR IN YOUR C.A.T. SCAN.
HERE'S AN X-RAY OF A TYPICAL BRAIN. EACH AREA SERVES A SPECIFIC NEED SUCH AS MOTOR SKILLS, THOUGHT PROCESSES.
WHAT WE'RE TRYING TO DETERMINE IS IF THERE IS A RELATIONSHIP BETWEEN YOUR RECENT BLACKOUT AND THE COLD YOU HAD. SEE SOME VIRUSES TRIGGER CERTAIN CHEMICAL REACTIONS IN OUR BODIES.
YOURS MAY HAVE SOMEHOW BLOCKED SOME NERVE IMPULSES FROM DOING THEIR JOB. IT'LL SHOW UP AS A CLOUDY AREA, LIKE THIS.
WE NEED YOUR SCANS TO MAKE ANY SORT OF JUDGMENT. SO, IF YOU'LL FOLLOW ME, THE LAB IS NOW READY FOR YOU.
WE'LL HAVE ALL THE RESULTS BACK IN A FEW DAYS.
A FEW DAYS?! I'VE ALREADY LIED TO WANDA ABOUT ALL THIS, HOPING IT'D JUST BLOW OVER.
"NOW I HAVE TO KEEP THIS UP SOME MORE."
UM... NO, I'M SORRY, WANDA, HE'S IN A MEETING. HE SHOULD BE BACK IN A COUPLE HOURS.
I'LL TELL HIM YOU PHONED.
THANKS, JULIA.
THAT'S STRANGE. HE NEVER MENTIONED A MEETING THIS MORNING.

NEW YORK CITY. THE CONCRETE JUNGLE.
WITHIN THE JUNGLE NOW LURKS THE BEAST.
HE'S MADE IT. AFTER A JOURNEY OF NEARLY A MONTH, HE NOW SMELLS THE STENCH OF MAN.
BUT IT'S ONE IN PARTICULAR WHOSE BLOOD HE SEEKS.
SIM-ONZ

IT'S BEEN A HELL OF A WEEK FOR TERRY. TWO SECURITY SYSTEMS OVERHAULED. DOZENS OF INTERLACED PHONE CONVERSATIONS. ANXIETY OVER TEST RESULTS.
AND ALL THE WHILE RECONSTRUCTING JASON WYNN'S MURDER CONSPIRACY AGAINST HIM.

THE ONLY THING I STILL CAN'T FIGURE IS WHY HE'D TRANSFER ME TO HIS OFFICE AFTER THE WHOLE INCIDENT BLEW OVER. HE CERTAINLY KNOWS I DON'T HAVE ANY POWER OVER HIM.
WELL, WHATEVER HE'S PLANNING, IT'S ABOUT TO GET CLIPPED.

I JUST WISH I DIDN'T FEEL SO TIRED. NOW'S NOT THE TIME TO FEEL WEAK. I'M ABOUT TO WALK INTO THE MIDDLE OF A MINEFIELD.
THE WORLD BEGINS TO SPIN AS HIS MIND WANDERS. IMAGES DISTORT. HE BLINKS FRANTICALLY, TRYING TO REGAIN HIS FOCUS.
IT ONLY GETS WORSE.

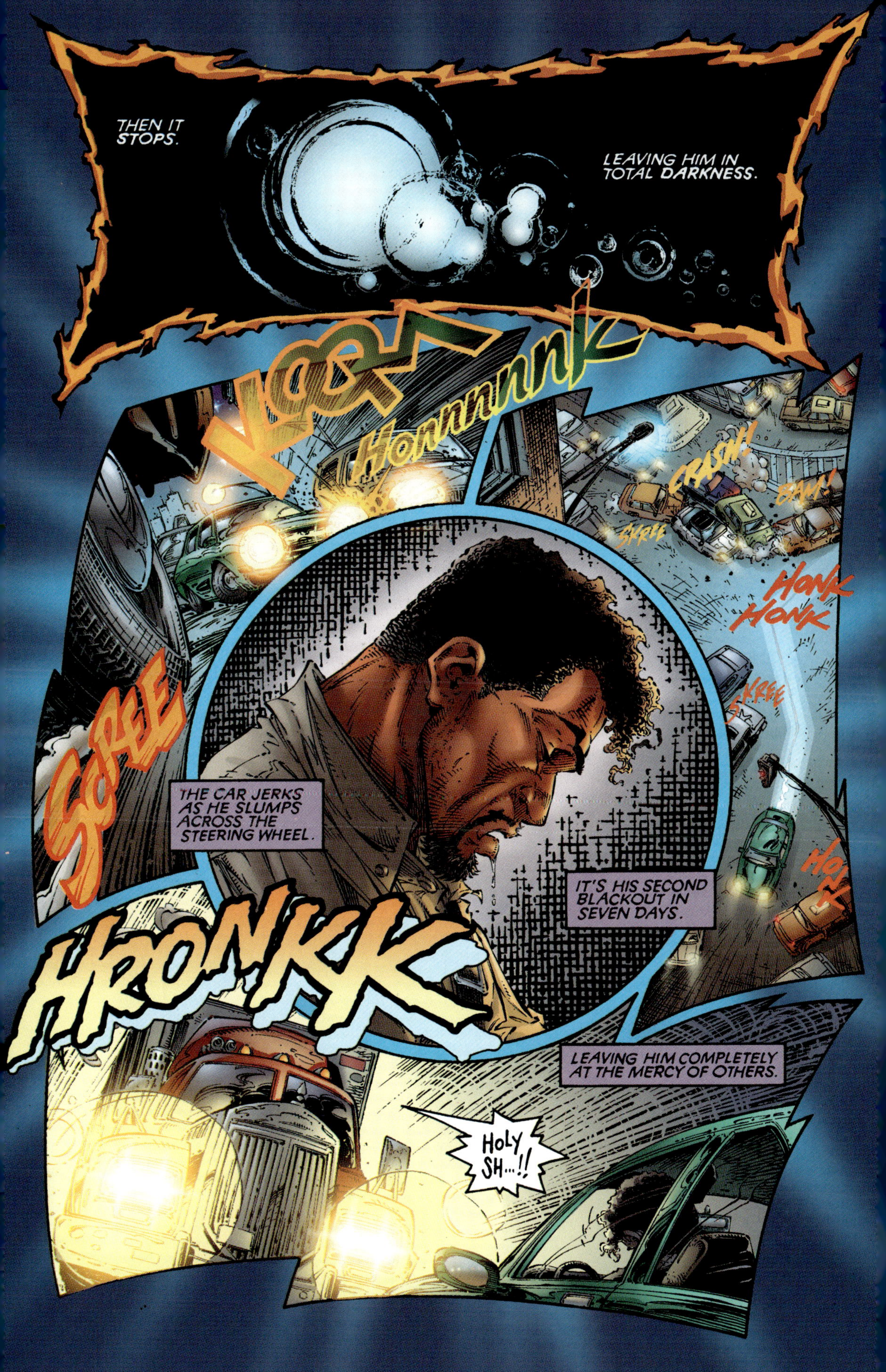

THEN IT STOPS.
LEAVING HIM IN TOTAL DARKNESS.
KOOM
Honnnnk
CRASH!
BAM!
SKREE
HONK HONK
SKREE
SCREE
THE CAR JERKS AS HE SLUMPS ACROSS THE STEERING WHEEL.
IT'S HIS SECOND BLACKOUT IN SEVEN DAYS.
HRONKK
LEAVING HIM COMPLETELY AT THE MERCY OF OTHERS.
HOLY SH...!!

uh...
what?
HE TRIES TO REACT.
TOO LATE.
KRASH
THEN ALL GOES DARK AGAIN.

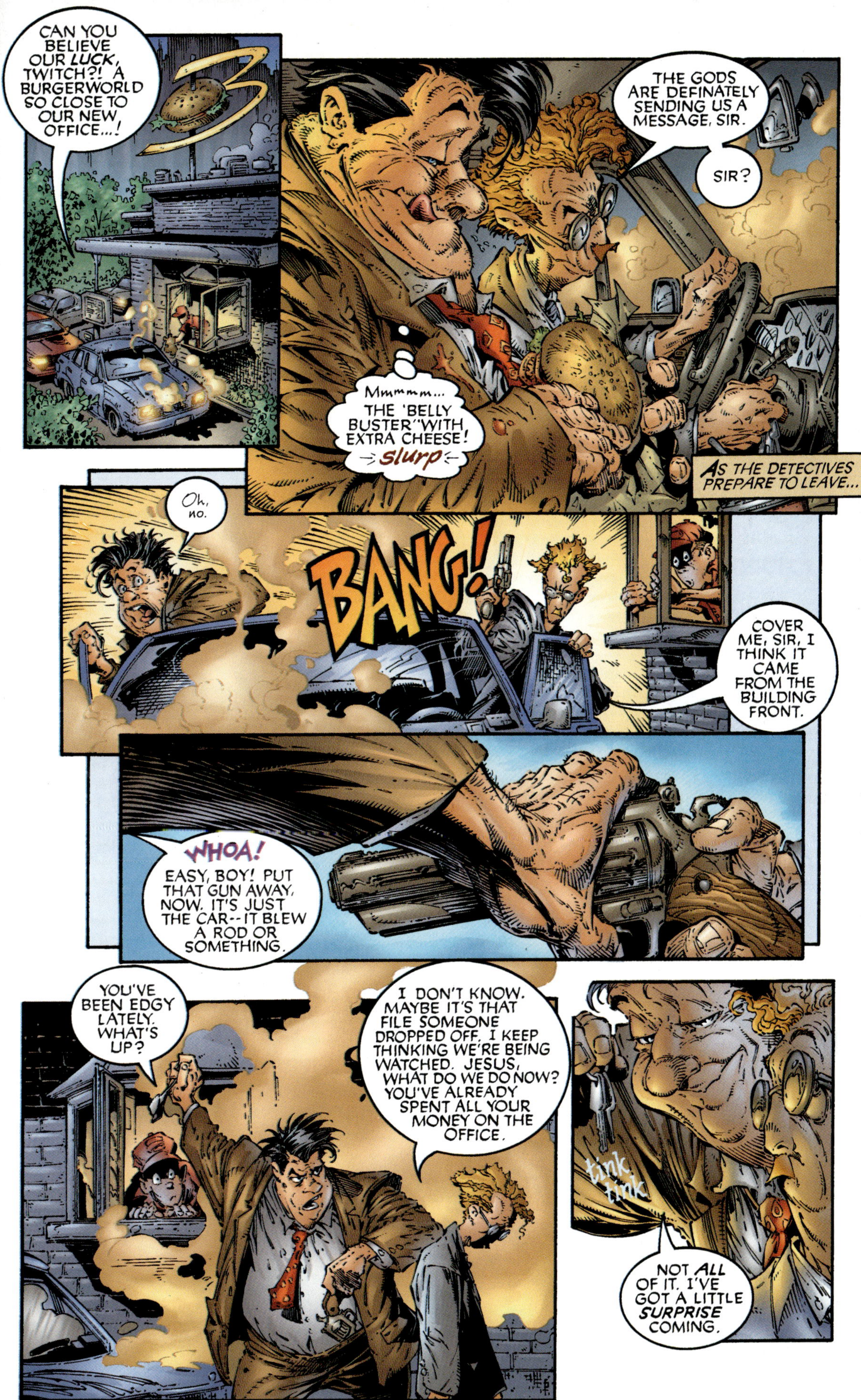

CAN YOU BELIEVE OUR LUCK, TWITCH?! A BURGERWORLD SO CLOSE TO OUR NEW OFFICE...!
THE GODS ARE DEFINATELY SENDING US A MESSAGE, SIR.
SIR?
Mmmmm... THE 'BELLY BUSTER" WITH EXTRA CHEESE! →Slurp←
AS THE DETECTIVES PREPARE TO LEAVE...
Oh, no.
BANG!
COVER ME, SIR, I THINK IT CAME FROM THE BUILDING FRONT.
WHOA! EASY, BOY! PUT THAT GUN AWAY, NOW. IT'S JUST THE CAR--IT BLEW A ROD OR SOMETHING.
YOU'VE BEEN EDGY LATELY. WHAT'S UP?
I DON'T KNOW. MAYBE IT'S THAT FILE SOMEONE DROPPED OFF, I KEEP THINKING WE'RE BEING WATCHED. JESUS, WHAT DO WE DO NOW? YOU'VE ALREADY SPENT ALL YOUR MONEY ON THE OFFICE.
tink, tink
NOT ALL OF IT. I'VE GOT A LITTLE SURPRISE COMING.

BRIING
BRIING
HELLO?
THIS IS SGT. FRITSCH OF THE NEW YORK CITY POLICE, MA'AM. ARE YOU WANDA BLAKE, TERRY FITZGERALD'S WIFE?
I'M SORRY, MA'AM, BUT YOUR HUSBAND'S BEEN IN AN ACCIDENT. IT'S PRETTY BAD.
HE WAS RUSHED TO ST. LUKE'S HOSPITAL ABOUT TWENTY MINUTES AGO. YOU MAY WANT TO...
HELLO?
HELLO? MA'AM?
YES. WHY? WHAT'S WRONG?
CLUNK
clatter

SPAWN
image
50
JUNE
$3.95
$5.50 CANADA
McFARLANE

AT FIRST, HE THOUGH IT WAS JUST A SIMPLE COLD. SOON IT DEVELOPED INTO SEVERE HACKING. NEITHER SEEMED OUT OF THE ORDINARY.
WHY WOULD THEY?
THEN CAME DIZZINESS, FOLLOWED BY A FAINTING SPELL. THAT'S WHEN HE STARTED TO GET ANXIOUS.
HIS FAMILY DOCTOR SENT HIM TO A SPECIALIST. THAT WAS A WEEK AGO. NO ONE KNEW. NOT HIS EMPLOYER, HIS FRIENDS OR HIS OWN FAMILY.
ON HIS DRIVE HOME TONIGHT, TERRY FITZGERALD EXPERIENCED HIS SECOND BLACKOUT. HE WAS AT HIS DESK FOR THE FIRST ONE.
THIS TIME HE WASN'T AS LUCKY.
IT WAS TRAVELLING AT 40 MILES PER HOUR WHEN THE ONCOMING TRUCK TRIED TO BRAKE. THERE WASN'T TIME.
THE DELIVERY TRUCK COLLIDED WITH TERRY.
HEAD ON.

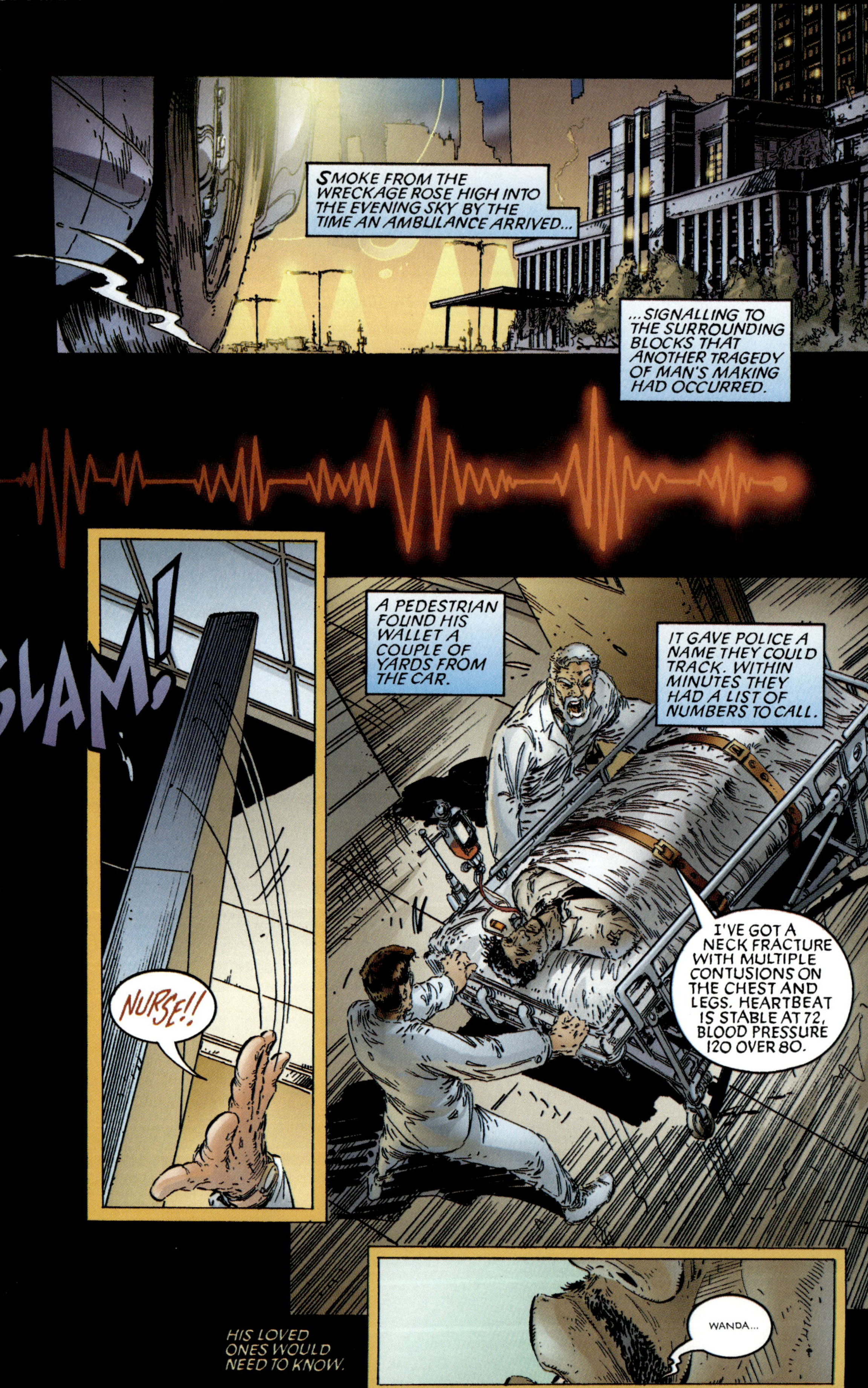

SMOKE FROM THE WRECKAGE ROSE HIGH INTO THE EVENING SKY BY THE TIME AN AMBULANCE ARRIVED...
...SIGNALLING TO THE SURROUNDING BLOCKS THAT ANOTHER TRAGEDY OF MAN'S MAKING HAD OCCURRED.
SLAM!
A PEDESTRIAN FOUND HIS WALLET A COUPLE OF YARDS FROM THE CAR.
IT GAVE POLICE A NAME THEY COULD TRACK. WITHIN MINUTES THEY HAD A LIST OF NUMBERS TO CALL.
NURSE!!
I'VE GOT A NECK FRACTURE WITH MULTIPLE CONTUSIONS ON THE CHEST AND LEGS. HEARTBEAT IS STABLE AT 72, BLOOD PRESSURE 120 OVER 80.
HIS LOVED ONES WOULD NEED TO KNOW.
WANDA...

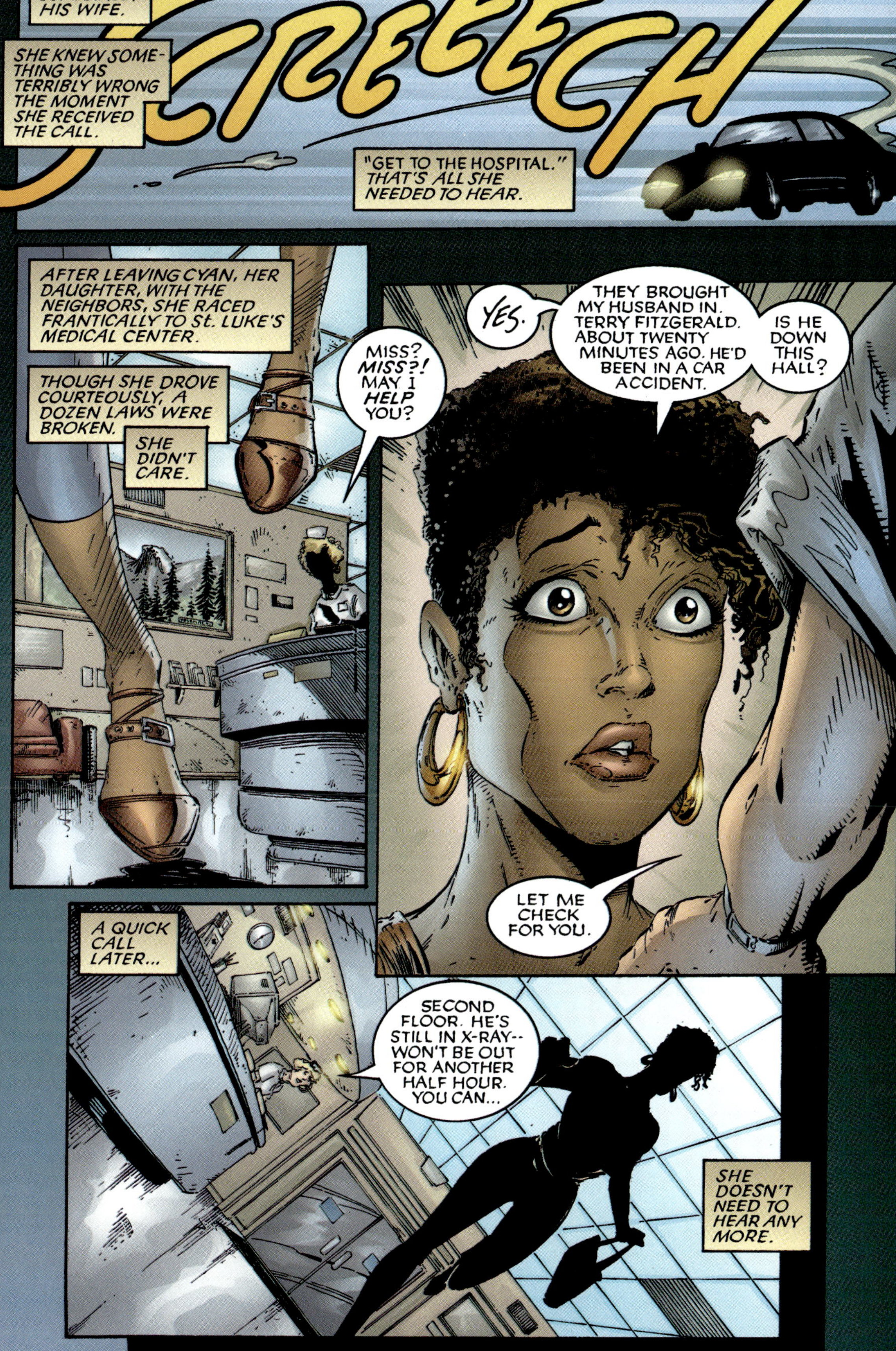

ESPECIALLY HIS WIFE.

SHE KNEW SOMETHING WAS TERRIBLY WRONG THE MOMENT SHE RECEIVED THE CALL.

SCREEECH

"GET TO THE HOSPITAL." THAT'S ALL SHE NEEDED TO HEAR.

AFTER LEAVING CYAN, HER DAUGHTER, WITH THE NEIGHBORS, SHE RACED FRANTICALLY TO ST. LUKE'S MEDICAL CENTER.

THOUGH SHE DROVE COURTEOUSLY, A DOZEN LAWS WERE BROKEN.

SHE DIDN'T CARE.

MISS? MISS?! MAY I HELP YOU?

YES.

THEY BROUGHT MY HUSBAND IN. TERRY FITZGERALD. ABOUT TWENTY MINUTES AGO. HE'D BEEN IN A CAR ACCIDENT.

IS HE DOWN THIS HALL?

LET ME CHECK FOR YOU.

A QUICK CALL LATER...

SECOND FLOOR. HE'S STILL IN X-RAY-- WON'T BE OUT FOR ANOTHER HALF HOUR. YOU CAN...

SHE DOESN'T NEED TO HEAR ANY MORE.

... SO, ALL IN ALL, IT APPEARS YOUR HUSBAND WAS VERY FORTUNATE THIS TIME. HIS SPRAINED ANKLE SHOULD BE FINE IN A FEW DAYS, BUT THE NECK BRACE WILL NEED TO STAY ON FOR AWHILE.
YOUR CAR'S SEATBELT AND AIRBAG JUST DID BOTH OF YOU A HUGE FAVOR.
ANYTHING ELSE, Dr. CURTIS?
NOT REALLY. BUT SINCE THIS IS HIS SECOND BLACKOUT...
SECOND?
... I'VE PUT A RUSH REQUEST ON THE RESULTS OF THAT C.A.T SCAN Dr. ROLLINS DID LAST WEEK.*
WHAT TEST?! WHEN DID YOU...
OH-oh.
*ISSUE 19.--Tom.
HEE HEE... um, YOU SEE, WANDA, I DIDN'T WANT YOU TO GET WORRIED ABOUT A LITTLE TESTING.
I'M A DEAD DUCK.
YOU KNOW ME. ALWAYS LOOKING OUT FOR YOUR BEST INTERESTS. I KNOW HOW KOOKY YOU CAN GET.

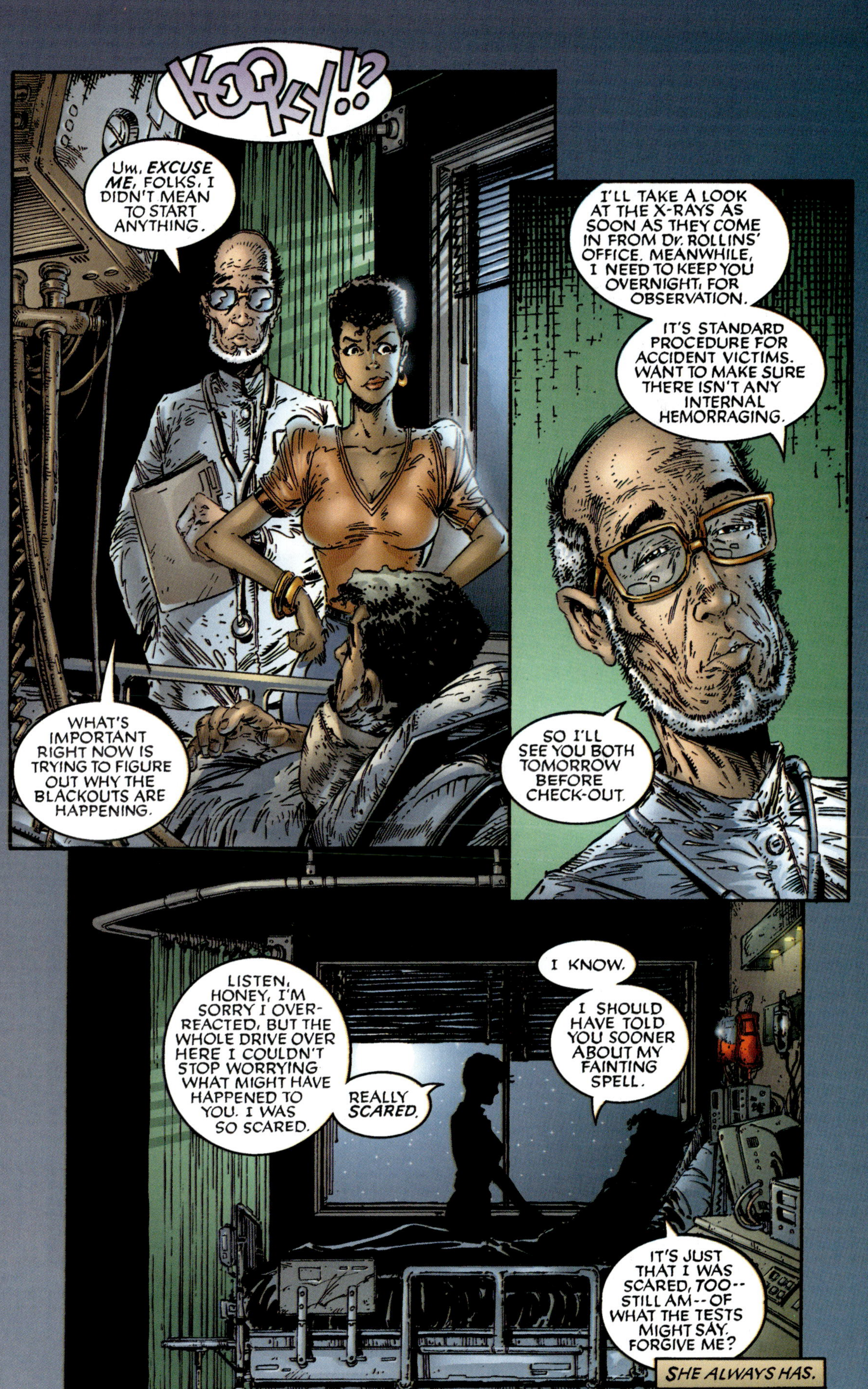
KOOKY!?
Um, EXCUSE ME, FOLKS, I DIDN'T MEAN TO START ANYTHING.
WHAT'S IMPORTANT RIGHT NOW IS TRYING TO FIGURE OUT WHY THE BLACKOUTS ARE HAPPENING.
I'LL TAKE A LOOK AT THE X-RAYS AS SOON AS THEY COME IN FROM Dr. ROLLINS' OFFICE. MEANWHILE, I NEED TO KEEP YOU OVERNIGHT, FOR OBSERVATION.
IT'S STANDARD PROCEDURE FOR ACCIDENT VICTIMS. WANT TO MAKE SURE THERE ISN'T ANY INTERNAL HEMORRAGING.
SO I'LL SEE YOU BOTH TOMORROW BEFORE CHECK-OUT.
LISTEN, HONEY, I'M SORRY I OVER-REACTED, BUT THE WHOLE DRIVE OVER HERE I COULDN'T STOP WORRYING WHAT MIGHT HAVE HAPPENED TO YOU. I WAS SO SCARED.
REALLY SCARED.
I KNOW.
I SHOULD HAVE TOLD YOU SOONER ABOUT MY FAINTING SPELL.
IT'S JUST THAT I WAS SCARED, TOO-- STILL AM-- OF WHAT THE TESTS MIGHT SAY. FORGIVE ME?
SHE ALWAYS HAS.

SOMEWHERE IN THE SHADOWS...
YOUR RECENT SEPARATION FROM THE SYMBIOTE HAS ACCELERATED ITS EVOLUTION, WITHOUT ANY GUIDANCE FROM YOU. THIS IS A VERY SERIOUS PROBLEM.
YOU SEE, RIGHT NOW THE COSTUME IS RUNNING IN ALL DIRECTIONS AT ONCE. IT'S LOST. AND, LIKE ANYTHING ELSE THAT BECOMES LOST IT WANTS TO RETURN HOME.
TO HELL.
PRECISELY. AND SINCE YOU'RE ATTACHED TO IT, YOU'RE GOING ALONG FOR THE RIDE.
IT'S RECONFIGURING ITSELF AT A TREMENDOUS RATE. USUALLY, THE METAMORPHOSIS TAKES YEARS TO COMPLETE.
AND THAT'S ONLY IF THE COSTUME AND ITS HOST ARE IN SYNC... WHICH YOU TWO DEFINATELY AREN'T.
SO WHAT CAN I DO?

DON'T TRIGGER IT. IT *FEEDS* OFF YOU-- YOUR *EVIL*. WHEN IT CAN'T DRAIN FROM YOU, THE *WORMS* BECOME THE CATALYST.
SO NOW I'M MADE OF EVIL.
NOT EXACTLY, AL.
BUT YOUR *ANGER* EVIL AND SIN COME IN MANY FORMS, YET *ANGER* IS THE ULTIMATE PIPELINE. NOTHING GOOD HAS EVER COME FROM RAGE. YOU'VE BEEN MAD SINCE YOUR REBIRTH-- ALMOST *CONSTANTLY*. THAT'S WHAT'S *FEEDING* IT.
YOU HAVE TO LET IT GO. WHAT-*EVER* IS FESTERING INSIDE YOU, *LET IT GO! PLEASE*, FOR *ALL* OF US-- FIND SOME INNER PEACE. JUST *LET THE ANGER DIE*.
BEFORE YOU LEAVE, COG, I HAVE TO KNOW SOME-THING. WHO *ARE* YOU?
A REFLECTION OF YOU. WE'RE THE *SAME*, AL. WE *BOTH* USED TO BE REAL, A *LIFETIME* AGO.
IN SHORT... I'M A SPAWN.

CYAN, No!
C'MON NOW, MOMMY DOESN'T WANT YOU THROWING YOUR FOOD ALL OVER THE PLACE, OKAY?
I'm Spoiled

Oh·oh. Mess. Mommy, mess.
YOU'RE RIGHT. IT'S A BIG MESS.
LET'S GET DOWN NOW AND GET DRESSED.

WE HAVE TO GO PICK UP DADDY! HE GETS TO COME HOME TODAY AND PLAY WITH YOU. WON'T THAT BE FUN? YOU AND DADDY?
MMMPHF gmdm MMMtp! phttt
HOLD STILL! I NEED TO CLEAN YOUR FACE!

AS THEY LEAVE THE HOUSE, WANDA IS ABSOLUTELY BEAMING.
BOUNDLESS JOY INFORMS HER VERY BEING. BIRDS. THE SKY. EVERYTHING SEEMS SO WONDERFUL.
SHE THANKS GOD FOR ANSWERING HER PRAYERS.

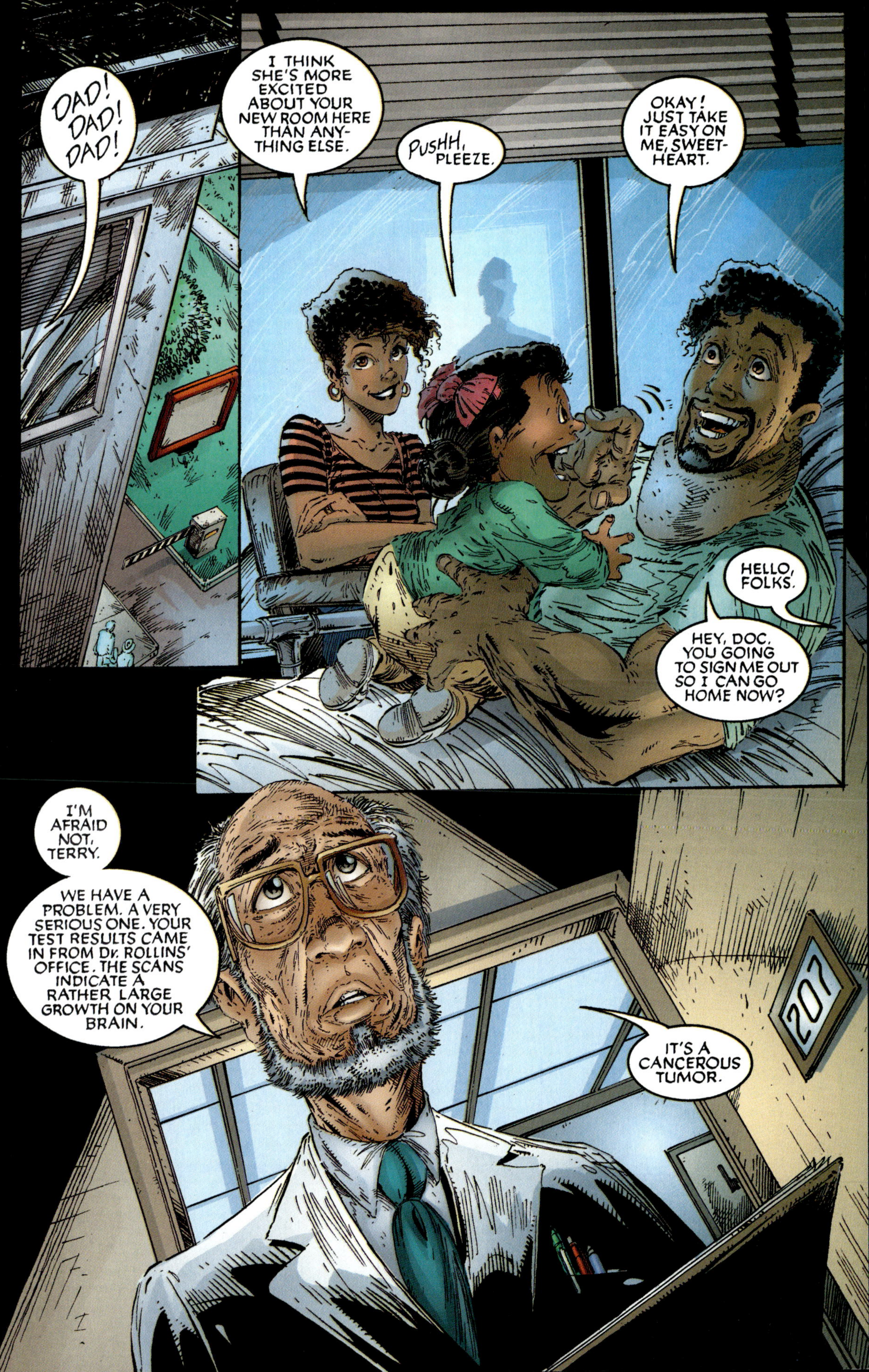

DAD! DAD! DAD!
I THINK SHE'S MORE EXCITED ABOUT YOUR NEW ROOM HERE THAN ANYTHING ELSE.
PUSHH, PLEEZE.
OKAY! JUST TAKE IT EASY ON ME, SWEETHEART.
HELLO, FOLKS.
HEY, DOC, YOU GOING TO SIGN ME OUT SO I CAN GO HOME NOW?
I'M AFRAID NOT, TERRY.
WE HAVE A PROBLEM. A VERY SERIOUS ONE. YOUR TEST RESULTS CAME IN FROM DR. ROLLINS' OFFICE. THE SCANS INDICATE A RATHER LARGE GROWTH ON YOUR BRAIN.
IT'S A CANCEROUS TUMOR.
207

IT CAN'T BE!!
YOU'RE KIDDING, RIGHT, DOC?
I WISH I WAS.
YOUR X-RAYS SHOW THE TUMOR NEAR THE BASE OF THE SKULL. IT'S ALREADY THE SIZE OF AN ORANGE, BUT THAT WILL SOON CHANGE.
WHAT'RE YOU SAYING? CAN'T YOU JUST OPERATE ON IT -- TAKE IT OUT...?
THAT'S WHAT WE'RE TRYING TO DETERMINE. UNFORTUNATELY, IT'S SHOWN UP IN AN AREA THAT USUALLY INDICATES AN ATTACHMENT. IF THE TUMOR IS MALIGNANT, DAMAGE TO THE BRAIN WOULD OCCUR IF WE WERE TO OPERATE.
SO, WHAT ARE MY OPTIONS?
LET US RUN SOME TESTS ON YOU -- DO A BIOPSY TO DETERMINE ITS RATE OF GROWTH... AND WHETHER IT'S MALIGNANT.
DADDY! GO HOME!
"IF IT IS...?"
"WE'LL DEAL WITH THAT LATER."

TWENTY HOURS AND A BATTERY OF TESTS LATER...
YOU SEE THIS CLOUDY AREA-- IT REPRESENTS THE CANCER.

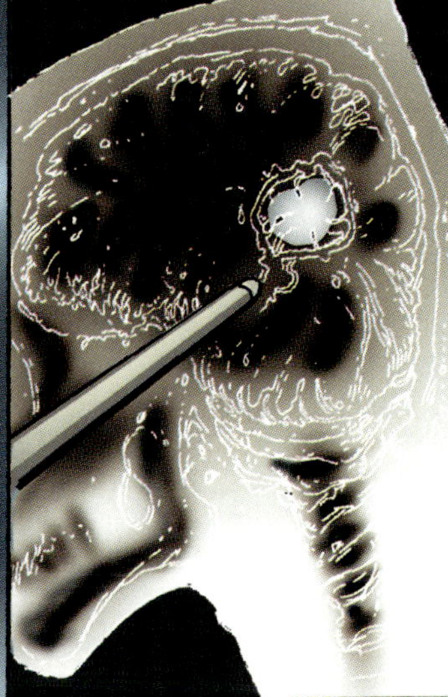

WHEN YOU HAD YOUR COLD, A VIRUS ENTERED YOUR SYSTEM. USUALLY, THE BODY COMBATS A VIRUS WITH A NUMBER OF DIFFERENT DEFENSES.
BUT AS YOUR COLD GOT WORSE, IT DEVELOPED INTO AN EARLY STAGE OF PNEUMONIA. AS THE VIRUS GREW STRONGER, IT TRIGGERED THE LATENT CELLS OF THE CANCER TO GROW.

MEANING YOU'VE ALWAYS HAD THIS IN YOU, JUST IN A DORMANT STATE. YOU, LIKE MILLIONS OF OTHERS, WERE PROBABLY BORN WITH IT.
UNFORTUNATELY, ITS POSITIONING MAKES IT IMPOSSIBLE FOR US TO OPERATE. TO REMOVE IT ALL, I'D HAVE TO REMOVE PART OF THE BRAIN, TOO. THIS IS COMPOUNDED BY THE FACT THAT THE TUMOR IS MALIGNANT.
MALIGNANT.
TERRY SQUEEZES WANDA EVEN HARDER.

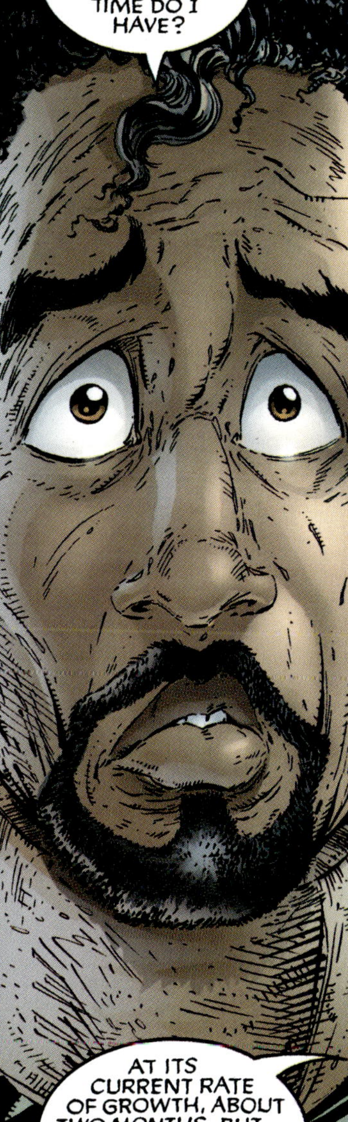

SO IT'D JUST GROW BACK, EVEN IF YOU COULD REMOVE IT.
YES.
MEANING I'M GOING TO DIE. ISN'T THAT RIGHT, DOCTOR? H-HOW MUCH TIME DO I HAVE?
AT ITS CURRENT RATE OF GROWTH, ABOUT TWO MONTHS, BUT THERE IS A SERIES OF PROCEDURES THAT CAN SLOW THE SPREAD OF IT.

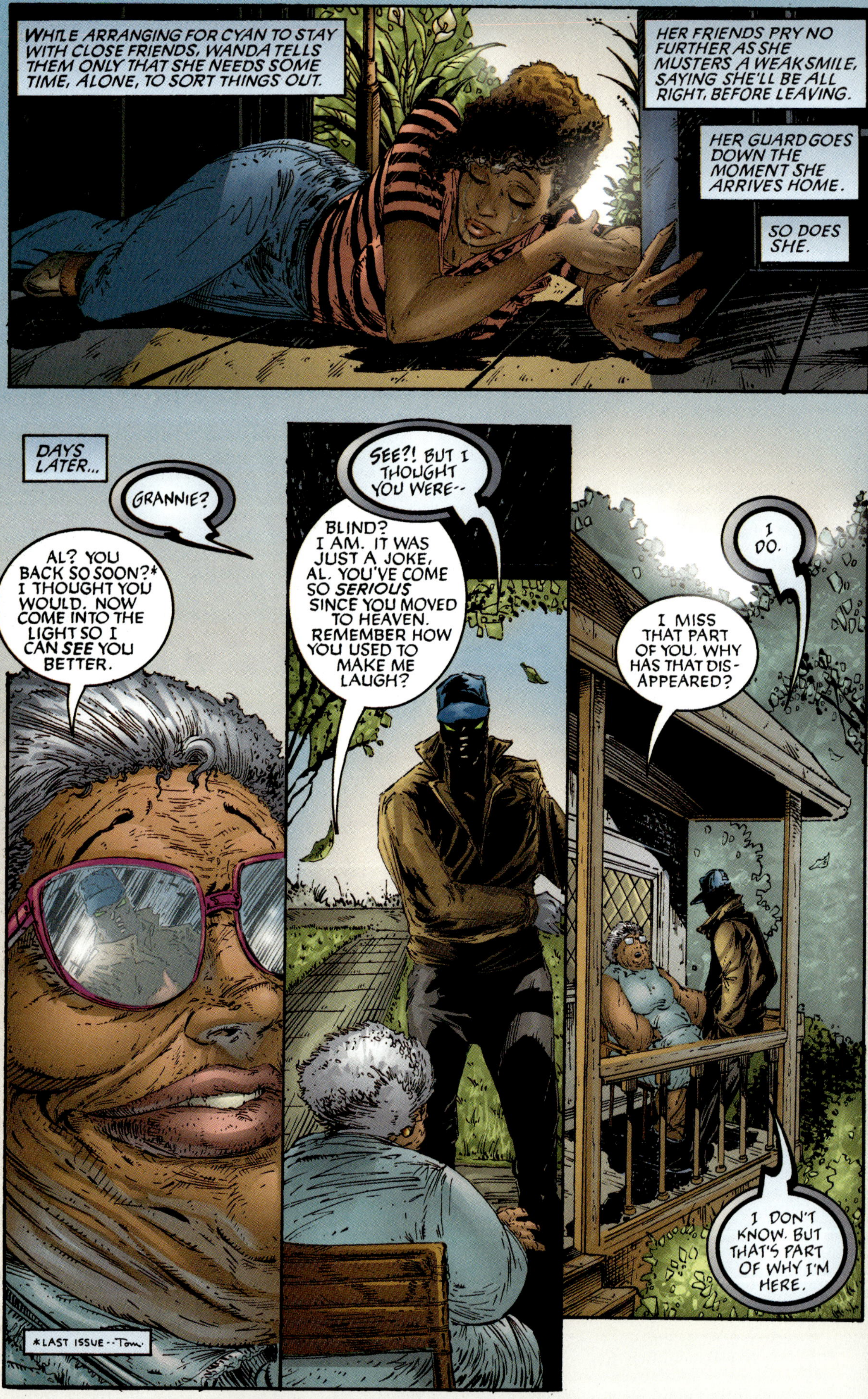

WHILE ARRANGING FOR CYAN TO STAY WITH CLOSE FRIENDS, WANDA TELLS THEM ONLY THAT SHE NEEDS SOME TIME, ALONE, TO SORT THINGS OUT.
HER FRIENDS PRY NO FURTHER AS SHE MUSTERS A WEAK SMILE, SAYING SHE'LL BE ALL RIGHT, BEFORE LEAVING.
HER GUARD GOES DOWN THE MOMENT SHE ARRIVES HOME.
SO DOES SHE.

DAYS LATER...
GRANNIE?
AL? YOU BACK SO SOON?* I THOUGHT YOU WOULD. NOW COME INTO THE LIGHT SO I CAN SEE YOU BETTER.
SEE?! BUT I THOUGHT YOU WERE--
BLIND? I AM. IT WAS JUST A JOKE, AL. YOU'VE COME SO SERIOUS SINCE YOU MOVED TO HEAVEN. REMEMBER HOW YOU USED TO MAKE ME LAUGH?
I DO.
I MISS THAT PART OF YOU. WHY HAS THAT DISAPPEARED?
I DON'T KNOW. BUT THAT'S PART OF WHY I'M HERE.
*LAST ISSUE--TOM.

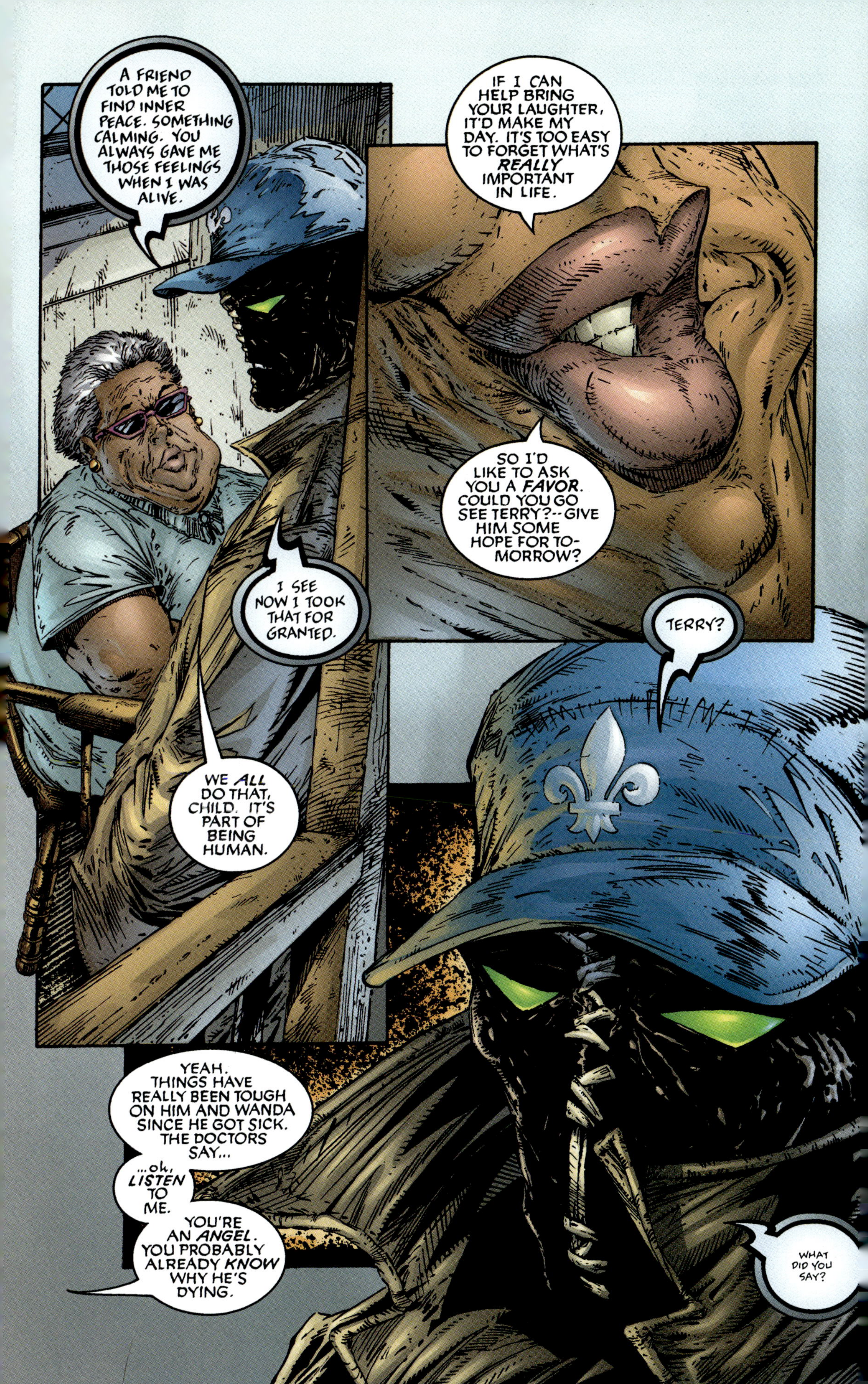

A FRIEND TOLD ME TO FIND INNER PEACE. SOMETHING CALMING. YOU ALWAYS GAVE ME THOSE FEELINGS WHEN I WAS ALIVE.
IF I CAN HELP BRING YOUR LAUGHTER, IT'D MAKE MY DAY. IT'S TOO EASY TO FORGET WHAT'S REALLY IMPORTANT IN LIFE.
SO I'D LIKE TO ASK YOU A FAVOR. COULD YOU GO SEE TERRY?-- GIVE HIM SOME HOPE FOR TO-MORROW?
I SEE NOW I TOOK THAT FOR GRANTED.
WE ALL DO THAT, CHILD. IT'S PART OF BEING HUMAN.
TERRY?
YEAH. THINGS HAVE REALLY BEEN TOUGH ON HIM AND WANDA SINCE HE GOT SICK. THE DOCTORS SAY...
...oh, LISTEN TO ME. YOU'RE AN ANGEL. YOU PROBABLY ALREADY KNOW WHY HE'S DYING.
WHAT DID YOU SAY?

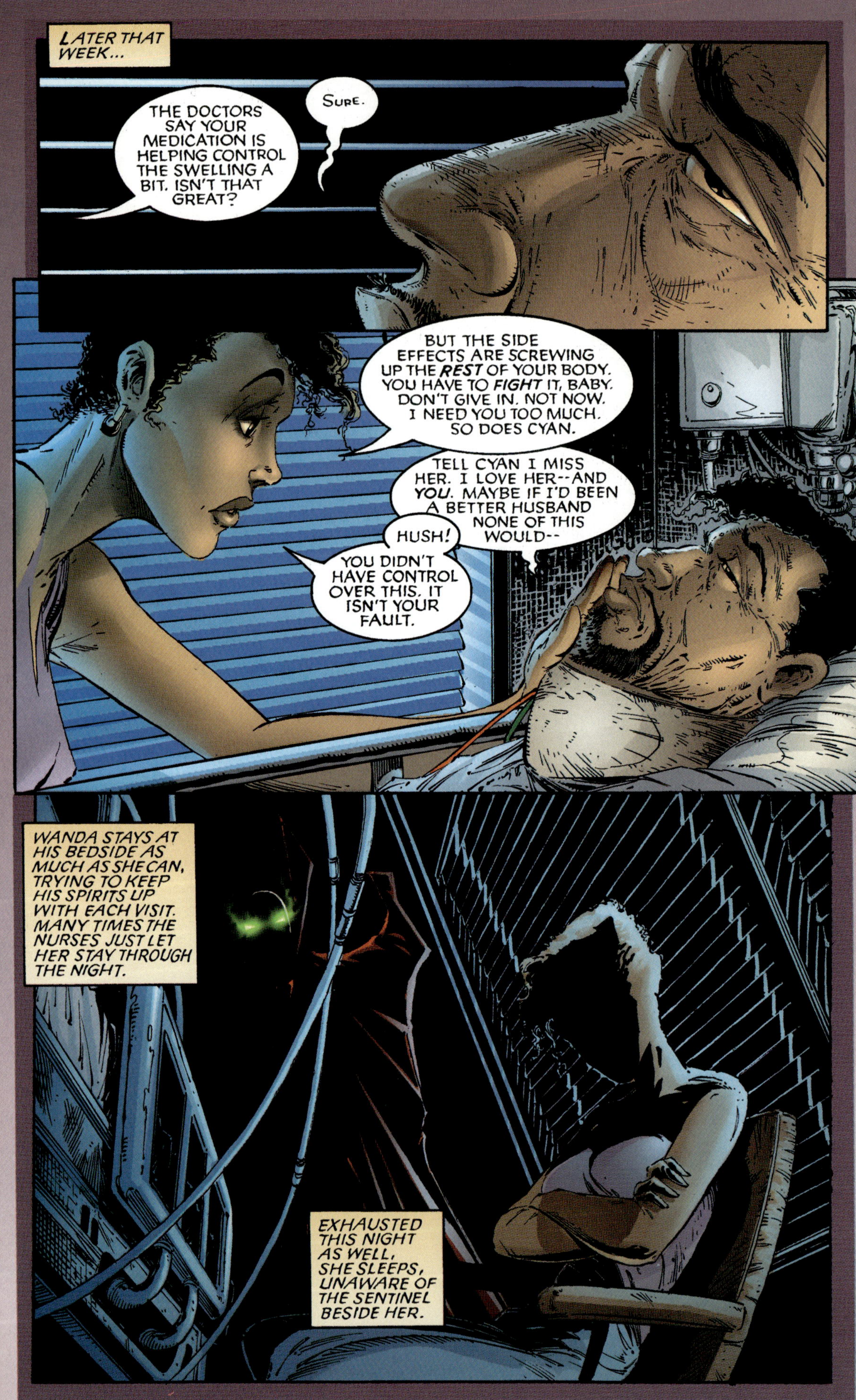

LATER THAT WEEK...
THE DOCTORS SAY YOUR MEDICATION IS HELPING CONTROL THE SWELLING A BIT. ISN'T THAT GREAT?
SURE.
BUT THE SIDE EFFECTS ARE SCREWING UP THE REST OF YOUR BODY. YOU HAVE TO FIGHT IT, BABY. DON'T GIVE IN. NOT NOW. I NEED YOU TOO MUCH. SO DOES CYAN.
TELL CYAN I MISS HER. I LOVE HER--AND YOU. MAYBE IF I'D BEEN A BETTER HUSBAND NONE OF THIS WOULD--
HUSH!
YOU DIDN'T HAVE CONTROL OVER THIS. IT ISN'T YOUR FAULT.
WANDA STAYS AT HIS BEDSIDE AS MUCH AS SHE CAN, TRYING TO KEEP HIS SPIRITS UP WITH EACH VISIT. MANY TIMES THE NURSES JUST LET HER STAY THROUGH THE NIGHT.
EXHAUSTED THIS NIGHT AS WELL, SHE SLEEPS, UNAWARE OF THE SENTINEL BESIDE HER.

TERRY USED TO BE HIS BEST FRIEND.

BUT NO MORE.

TERRY STOLE HIS WIFE FROM HIM. GAVE HER THE CHILD HE NEVER COULD. PROTECTED THE MAN WHO ORDERED HIS DEATH.

WHY SHOULD HE HELP HIM-- ESPECIALLY NOW, WHEN HIS SYMBIOTE IS BEHAVING SO ERRATICALLY.

SINCE COMING BACK FROM THE DEAD AS A HELLSPAWN, AL HAS DISCOVERED HIS FRIEND'S TRUE SIDE.

THAT OF A TRAITOR.

COG TOLD HIM TO RELAX. NOT USE HIS POWERS.

AND HE WON'T. NOT FOR HIM. HE'S NOT WORTH GOING TO HELL FOR.

SO WHY DID HE COME?

TO GLOAT?

AND WHY DID HE SAVE TERRY AWHILE BACK?*

MAYBE HE DID WANT TO HELP... BUT NOT TO THE EXTENT OF MAKING THAT KIND OF SACRIFICE. NOT FOR TERRY.

CONFUSED, HE LEAVES.

*ISSUE 24 --Tom.

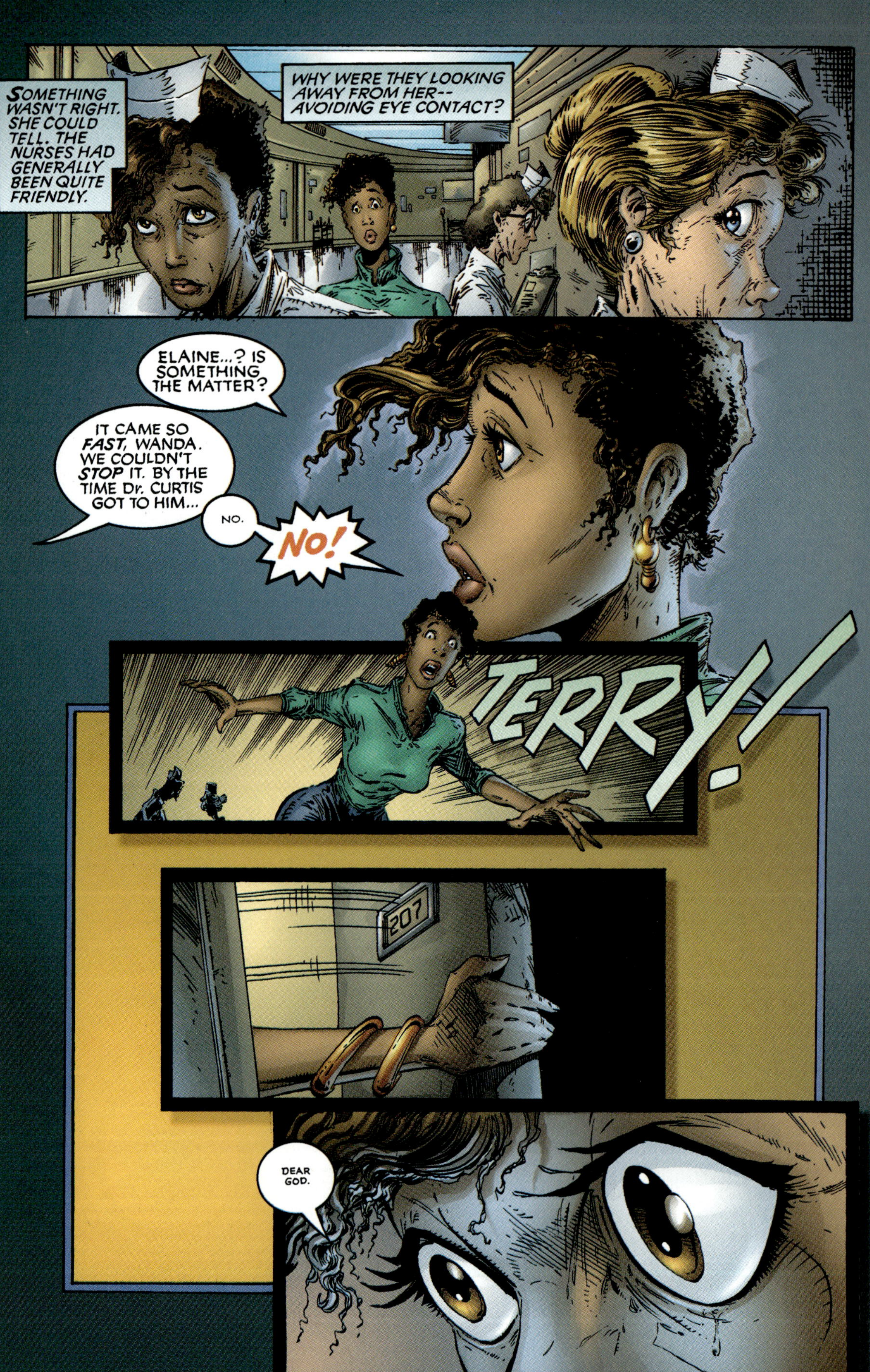

SOMETHING WASN'T RIGHT. SHE COULD TELL. THE NURSES HAD GENERALLY BEEN QUITE FRIENDLY.
WHY WERE THEY LOOKING AWAY FROM HER-- AVOIDING EYE CONTACT?
ELAINE...? IS SOMETHING THE MATTER?
IT CAME SO FAST, WANDA. WE COULDN'T STOP IT. BY THE TIME DR. CURTIS GOT TO HIM...
NO.
NO!
TERRY!
207
DEAR GOD.

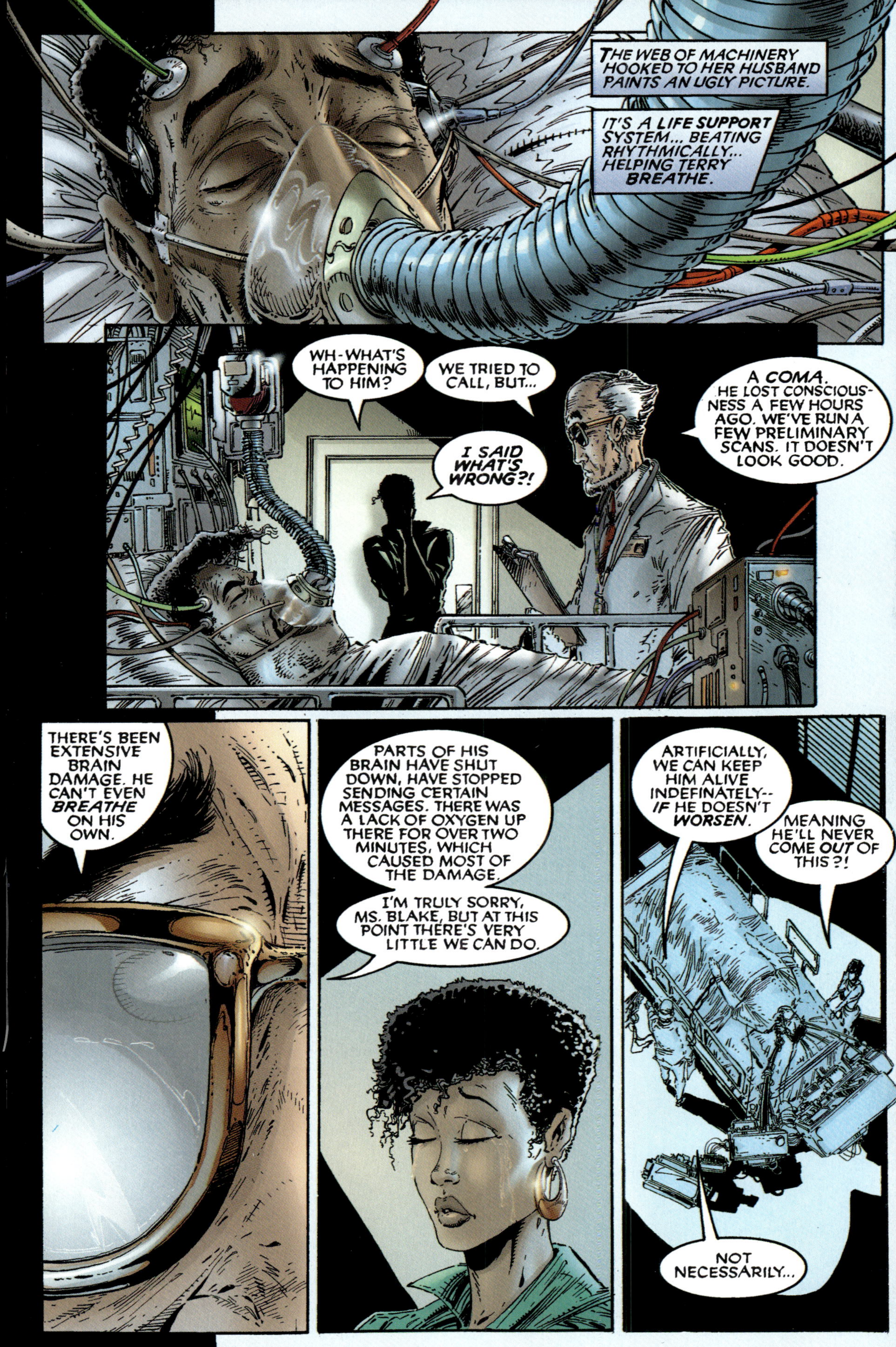

THE WEB OF MACHINERY HOOKED TO HER HUSBAND PAINTS AN UGLY PICTURE.
IT'S A LIFE SUPPORT SYSTEM... BEATING RHYTHMICALLY... HELPING TERRY BREATHE.
WH-WHAT'S HAPPENING TO HIM?
WE TRIED TO CALL, BUT...
I SAID WHAT'S WRONG?!
A COMA. HE LOST CONSCIOUSNESS A FEW HOURS AGO. WE'VE RUN A FEW PRELIMINARY SCANS. IT DOESN'T LOOK GOOD.
THERE'S BEEN EXTENSIVE BRAIN DAMAGE. HE CAN'T EVEN BREATHE ON HIS OWN.
PARTS OF HIS BRAIN HAVE SHUT DOWN, HAVE STOPPED SENDING CERTAIN MESSAGES. THERE WAS A LACK OF OXYGEN UP THERE FOR OVER TWO MINUTES, WHICH CAUSED MOST OF THE DAMAGE.
I'M TRULY SORRY, MS. BLAKE, BUT AT THIS POINT THERE'S VERY LITTLE WE CAN DO.
ARTIFICIALLY, WE CAN KEEP HIM ALIVE INDEFINATELY-- IF HE DOESN'T WORSEN.
MEANING HE'LL NEVER COME OUT OF THIS?!
NOT NECESSARILY...

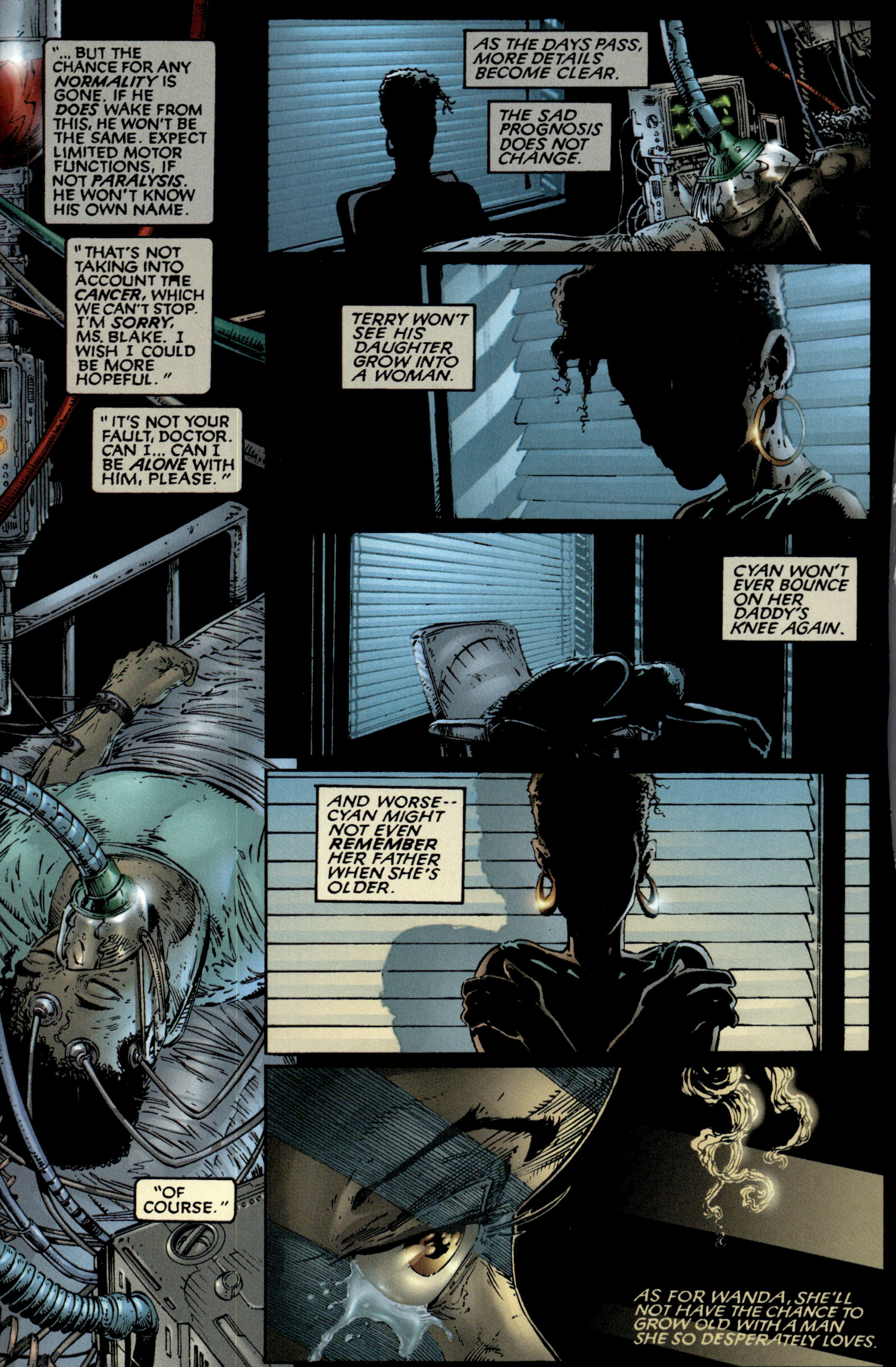
"...BUT THE CHANCE FOR ANY NORMALITY IS GONE. IF HE DOES WAKE FROM THIS, HE WON'T BE THE SAME. EXPECT LIMITED MOTOR FUNCTIONS, IF NOT PARALYSIS. HE WON'T KNOW HIS OWN NAME.
"THAT'S NOT TAKING INTO ACCOUNT THE CANCER, WHICH WE CAN'T STOP. I'M SORRY, MS. BLAKE. I WISH I COULD BE MORE HOPEFUL."
"IT'S NOT YOUR FAULT, DOCTOR. CAN I... CAN I BE ALONE WITH HIM, PLEASE."
AS THE DAYS PASS, MORE DETAILS BECOME CLEAR.
THE SAD PROGNOSIS DOES NOT CHANGE.
TERRY WON'T SEE HIS DAUGHTER GROW INTO A WOMAN.
CYAN WON'T EVER BOUNCE ON HER DADDY'S KNEE AGAIN.
AND WORSE-- CYAN MIGHT NOT EVEN REMEMBER HER FATHER WHEN SHE'S OLDER.
"OF COURSE."
AS FOR WANDA, SHE'LL NOT HAVE THE CHANCE TO GROW OLD WITH A MAN SHE SO DESPERATELY LOVES.

AT THE TENDER AGE OF TWENTY-NINE, WANDA SHOULD BE FULL OF LIFE, LOOKING FORWARD TO EACH NEW DAY AND ITS ENDLESS POSSIBILITIES.
NOT ANYMORE. FOR THE SECOND TIME, SHE WILL OUTLIVE HER HUSBAND -- ONE, KILLED IN THE LINE OF DUTY FIVE YEARS AGO, AND NOW ANOTHER, BEING EATEN ALIVE BY CANCER.
SO SHE RETREATS INWARD, SHUTTING HERSELF OFF FROM EVERYTHING. EVERYONE. IT'S THE ONLY WAY SHE HAS TO HANDLE HER PAIN:
...TO BECOME COMPLETELY NUMB TO IT ALL.
JUST LIKE HIM. HE'S LOST THE PRECIOUS THINGS, TOO.
HE TORTURES HIMSELF CONSTANTLY WITH HIS UNREALISTIC HOPES THAT HE CAN GET HER BACK AGAIN.

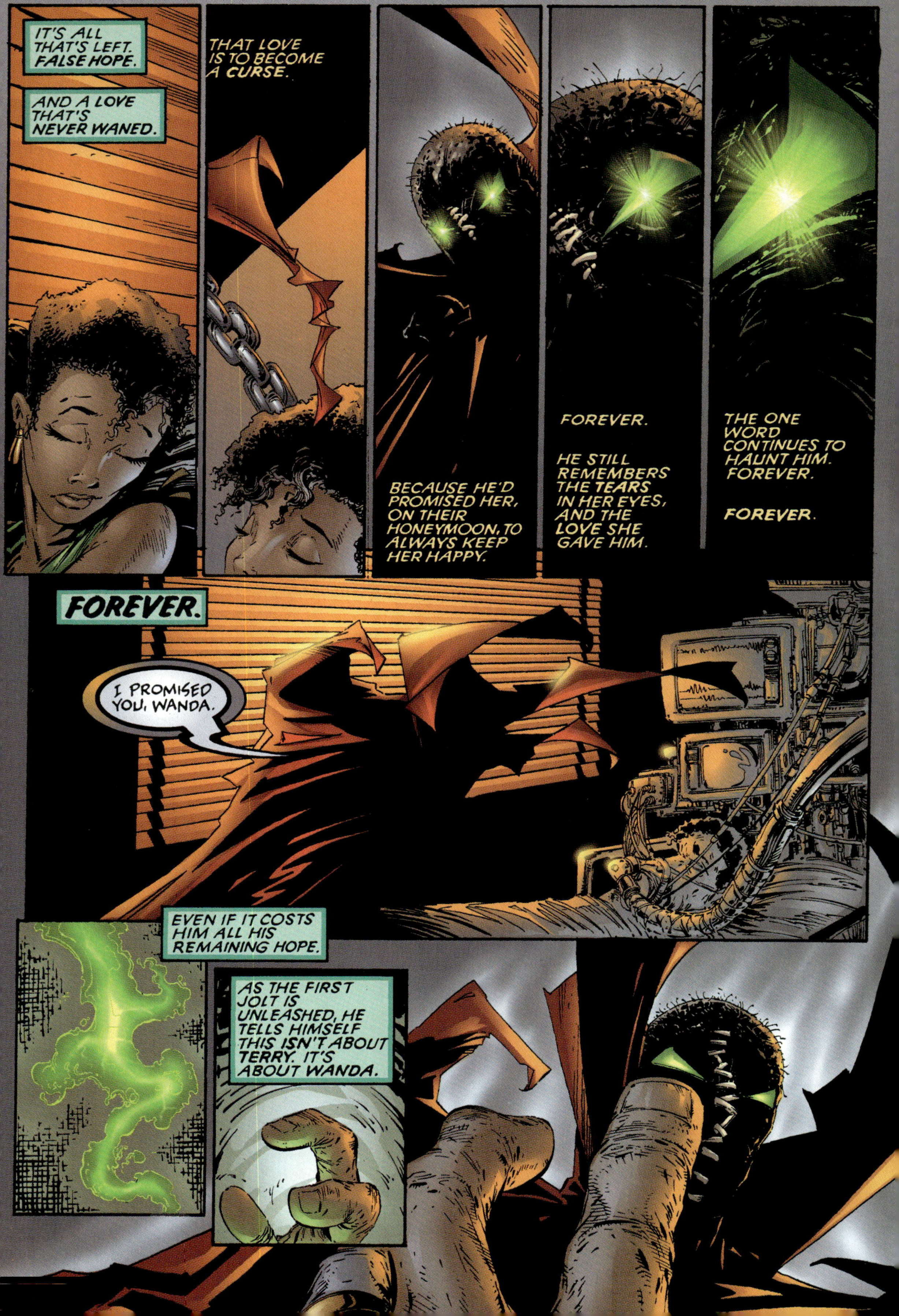

IT'S ALL THAT'S LEFT. FALSE HOPE.
AND A LOVE THAT'S NEVER WANED.

THAT LOVE IS TO BECOME A CURSE.

BECAUSE HE'D PROMISED HER, ON THEIR HONEYMOON, TO ALWAYS KEEP HER HAPPY.

FOREVER.
HE STILL REMEMBERS THE TEARS IN HER EYES, AND THE LOVE SHE GAVE HIM.

THE ONE WORD CONTINUES TO HAUNT HIM. FOREVER.
FOREVER.

FOREVER.
I PROMISED YOU, WANDA.
EVEN IF IT COSTS HIM ALL HIS REMAINING HOPE.
AS THE FIRST JOLT IS UNLEASHED, HE TELLS HIMSELF THIS ISN'T ABOUT TERRY. IT'S ABOUT WANDA.

TERRY'S BODY ARCHES AGAINST THE PAIN. A SPASTIC FINGER CATCHES THE LACING THAT HOLDS SPAWN'S FACE TOGETHER.
SPAWN BARELY NOTICES.
HE'S THINKING ABOUT HIS LIFE.
HIS WIFE.
THEY'LL NEVER BE TOGETHER AGAIN, SO ALL THAT MATTERS IS HER HAPPINESS-- AND HIS PROMISE.
IT'S TIME HE LET HER GO.
AL?
I USED TO BE.
HE HESITATES, THEN HEARS THE WORD AGAIN:
FOREVER!
THEN HE'S GONE... VANISHED TO GOD ONLY KNOWS WHERE.
uh...?

HELP!!
HELP ME!!
BZZT
BZZT
BZZT
THOSE SCREAMS...?!
OH, NO! I'VE GOT A FLAT LINE IN ROOM 207!
CODE BLUE!
ELAINE, GRAB A CRASH CART AND COME WITH ME-- STAT!
THEY'VE BEEN TRAINED FOR EVERY SITUATION POSSIBLE, THESE NURSES.
OR SO THEY THINK.
HELP!!
PLEASE, CAN SOMEBODY HELP MY WIFE...?
I THINK SHE'S FAINTED.
THE STAFF WILL SEARCH FOR ANSWERS TO THIS MIRACULOUS EVENT.
THEY WON'T FIND ANY CLUES.

3

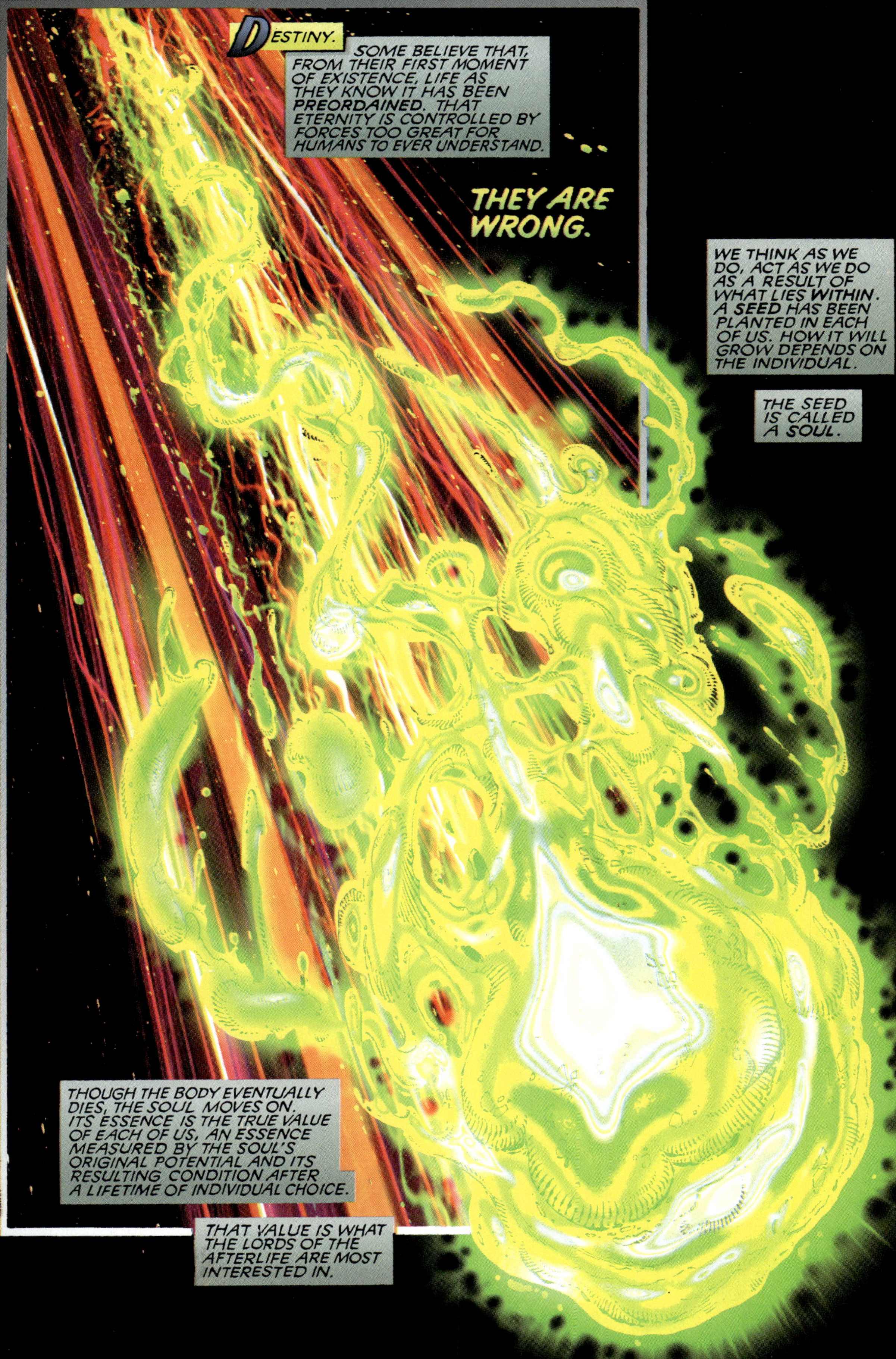

DESTINY. SOME BELIEVE THAT, FROM THEIR FIRST MOMENT OF EXISTENCE, LIFE AS THEY KNOW IT HAS BEEN PREORDAINED. THAT ETERNITY IS CONTROLLED BY FORCES TOO GREAT FOR HUMANS TO EVER UNDERSTAND.
THEY ARE WRONG.
WE THINK AS WE DO, ACT AS WE DO AS A RESULT OF WHAT LIES WITHIN. A SEED HAS BEEN PLANTED IN EACH OF US. HOW IT WILL GROW DEPENDS ON THE INDIVIDUAL.
THE SEED IS CALLED A SOUL.
THOUGH THE BODY EVENTUALLY DIES, THE SOUL MOVES ON. ITS ESSENCE IS THE TRUE VALUE OF EACH OF US, AN ESSENCE MEASURED BY THE SOUL'S ORIGINAL POTENTIAL AND ITS RESULTING CONDITION AFTER A LIFETIME OF INDIVIDUAL CHOICE.
THAT VALUE IS WHAT THE LORDS OF THE AFTERLIFE ARE MOST INTERESTED IN.

AT DEATH, EACH BEING MAKES THE SAME VOYAGE, WITH FRAGMENTED MEMORIES SPINNING IN THE VOID. THOSE SCATTERED IMPRESSIONS SHINE LIKE BEACONS, SENDING AN UNDOCTORED RESUME OF THAT INDIVIDUAL.
IT'S FROM THIS INFORMATION THAT WE ARE DEALT OUR FINAL JUDGMENT. OUR DESTINY.
THERE ARE ONLY TWO POSSIBLE OUTCOMES. HEAVEN OR HELL.
BY THIS POINT, WE ARE LOOKED UPON, NOT AS WHAT WE WERE AT DEATH, BUT AS WHAT WE MAY YET BECOME.
IN TERMS OF BOTH GOOD AND EVIL.

WITH HEAVEN AND HELL ALTERNATING CHOICES FROM AN ENDLESS POOL OF HUMANITY.

THE PICKS ARE BASED ON PERFORMANCE EXPECTATIONS. GETTING TO HEAVEN DOES NOT INDICATE A SPIRIT'S 'GOODNESS' ANY MORE THAN A SENTENCE TO HELL MEANS THERE IS AN 'EVILNESS.'

SOMETIMES THE DECISION IS MADE STRICTLY TO PREVENT THE OTHER SIDE FROM ACQUIRING ANOTHER VALUABLE PROPERTY.

IT'S UP TO GOD--OR SATAN--TO EXPLOIT EACH INDIVIDUAL'S STRENGTHS...

...OR WEAKNESSES.

FOR HELL, THE TWO EASIEST ARE ALWAYS REVENGE OR LOVE.

IT'S THE LATTER THAT DAMNED AL SIMMONS.

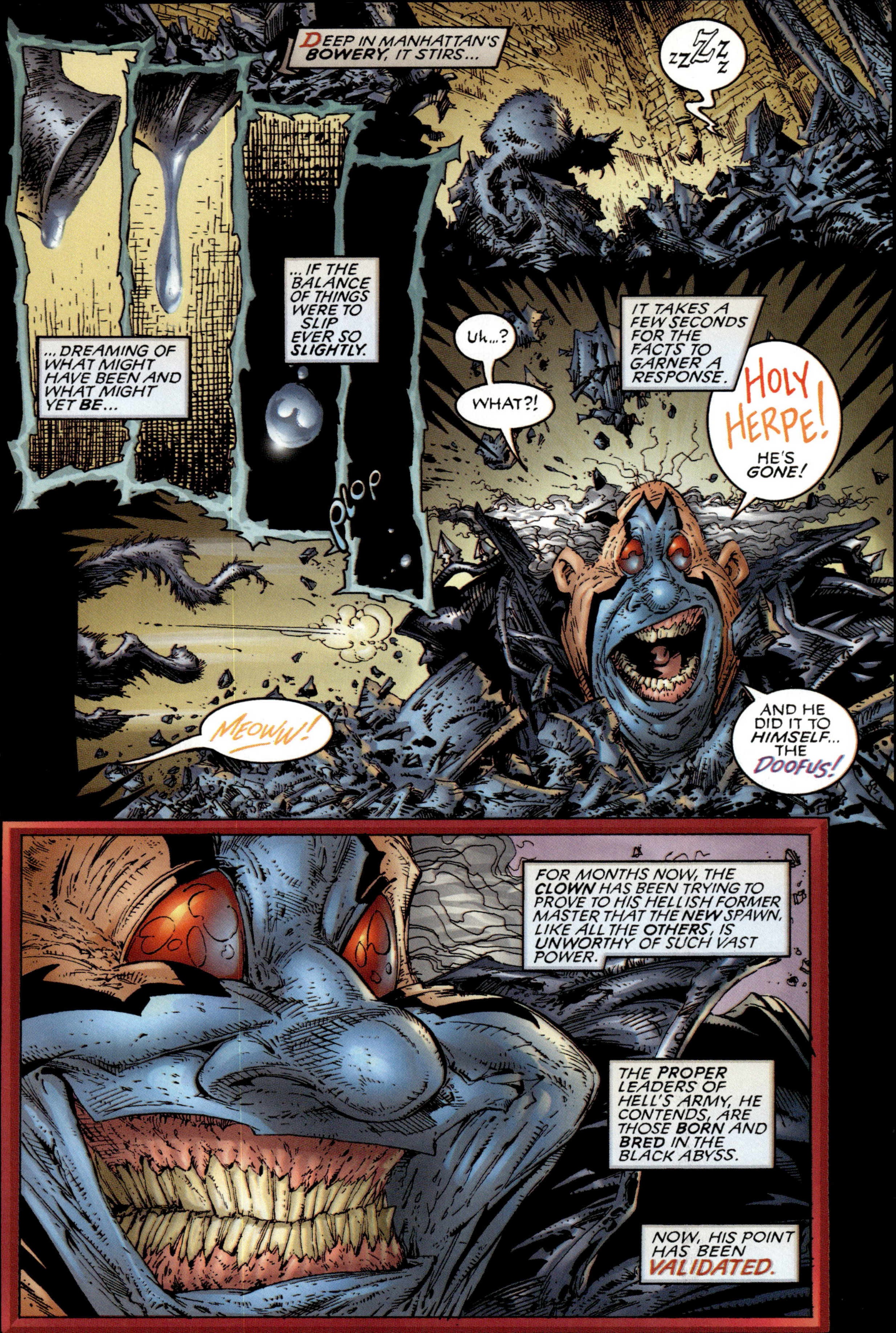

DEEP IN MANHATTAN'S BOWERY, IT STIRS...
...DREAMING OF WHAT MIGHT HAVE BEEN AND WHAT MIGHT YET BE...
...IF THE BALANCE OF THINGS WERE TO SLIP EVER SO SLIGHTLY.
PLOP
MEOWW!
ZZZZZ
UH...?
WHAT?!
IT TAKES A FEW SECONDS FOR THE FACTS TO GARNER A RESPONSE.
HOLY HERPE!
HE'S GONE!
AND HE DID IT TO HIMSELF... THE DOOFUS!
FOR MONTHS NOW, THE CLOWN HAS BEEN TRYING TO PROVE TO HIS HELLISH FORMER MASTER THAT THE NEW SPAWN, LIKE ALL THE OTHERS, IS UNWORTHY OF SUCH VAST POWER.
THE PROPER LEADERS OF HELL'S ARMY, HE CONTENDS, ARE THOSE BORN AND BRED IN THE BLACK ABYSS.
NOW, HIS POINT HAS BEEN VALIDATED.

FOR CENTURIES THIS CREATURE, ONCE HONORED WITH THE TASK OF CHAPERONING EACH OF MALEBOLGIA'S NEW HELLSPAWN, HAS DREAMT OF THIS MOMENT.
FROLICING WITH SOILED DISCARDS AND ROTTED GARBAGE, HIS CELEBRATION REACHES FEVER PITCH.
THEN COMES A THOUGHT--
--AND WITH IT, THE LOSS OF ANY JOY.
WAIT A MINUTE!
SIMMONS IS BACK IN HELL, BUT I DIDN'T PUT HIM THERE! HE SCREWED HIMSELF UP, LIKE A LOT OF THE OTHERS DID.
SO MALEBOLGIA WILL JUST FIND ANOTHER IN A CENTURY OR TWO.
CRAP.
THAT'S NOT WHAT I WANTED. HE NEEDS TO SEE THAT NO HUMAN SHOULD BE CHOSEN EVER AGAIN.
IT'S HIS OWN CHILDREN WHO SHOULD LEAD. WE ARE THE TRUE EVIL.
I NEED TO PROVE THAT TO HIM, ONCE AND FOR ALL...
...AND I KNOW JUST WHERE TO START.

A FEW DAYS LATER...
OUTPATIENT REGISTRATION
AFTERNOON MS. BLAKE.
HELLO, DOCTOR. YOU SAID YOU WANTED TO SEE ME.
YES. I JUST RECEIVED THE RESULTS OF THE LATEST TESTS. AND TO BE QUITE HONEST, THIS WHOLE SITUATION HAS EVERYONE COMPLETELY STUMPED.
THERE'S NO MORE EVIDENCE OF CANCER ANYWHERE IN HIS BODY. AS A MATTER OF FACT, THE AREA OF HIS HEAD WHICH WAS AFFECTED IS CLEANER THAN NORMAL. WE'VE RUN EVERY DIAGNOSTIC I CAN THINK OF. EACH RESULT IS NEGATIVE.
SO WHAT DOES THAT MEAN?
HOLY BIBLE

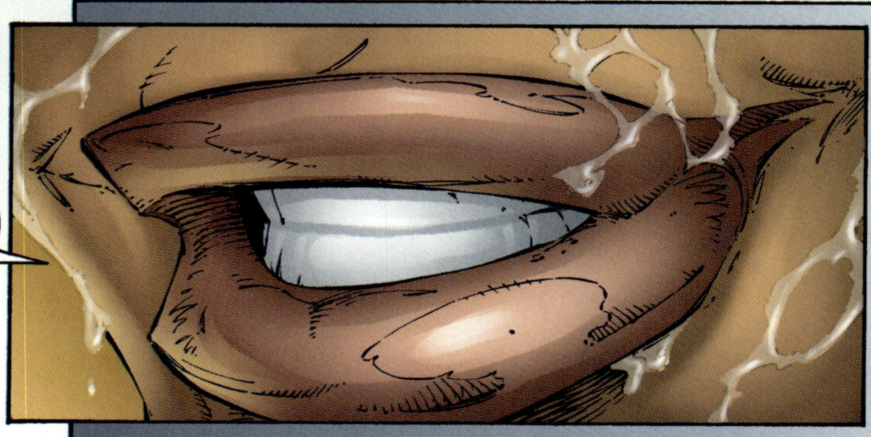

CALL IT A MIRACLE, BUT TERRY IS 100% CURED. SO, UNLESS EITHER ONE OF YOU HAS ANY OBJECTIONS...
...I'M RELEASING HIM TOMORROW. IT'S TIME HE WENT HOME TO HIS FAMILY.
THANK YOU, DOCTOR. AND IF YOU DON'T MIND, I'D LIKE TO TELL HIM MYSELF.
OF COURSE.

THE DRIVE HOME FOUND THEM WITH LITTLE TO SAY, AND, AS TERRY WIPED A FEW TEARS FROM HIS WIFE'S CHEEK, THE TWO OF THEM FELL SILENT. LOVING GLANCES SPOKE FOR THEM... OF AWE, AND RELIEF, AND THE CERTAINTY THAT BEING WITH EACH OTHER MEANS MORE THAN ANYTHING.
CYAN'S GOING TO BE SO HAPPY TO SEE HER DADDY BACK HOME.
JUST KNOWING I'LL GET TO SEE HER PRETTY FACE AS SHE GROWS UP-- AND YOURS AS WE GROW OLDER-- MAKES ANYTHING I'LL HAVE TO BEAR FROM NOW ON SEEM EASY.
I CAN'T BELIEVE HOW GOOD SHE BEHAVED AT THE HOSPITAL EACH TIME. SHE SURE...
CLICK
SURPRISE!!
FRIENDS. A THRONG OF PEOPLE WHO NEVER BELIEVED A WORD OF THE MURDER ACCUSA-TIONS GATHER NOW TO WELCOME HIM HOME.
TERRY LOOKS AT EACH OF THEM AND SMILES. HE'LL NEVER AGAIN TAKE TRUE FRIENDSHIP FOR GRANTED.

TERRY GOES ON GRINNING BROADLY FOR THE REST OF THE EVENING.
HE MAKES SURE CYAN DOESN'T FEEL FORGOTTEN BY RIDING HER ON HIS SHOULDERS MOST OF THE TIME.
AND EVEN WHILE INVOLVED IN CONVERSATIONS WITH EVERYONE IN REACH, HE CAN'T SEEM TO STOP GAZING AT JUST ONE SIGHT-- HIS WIFE.
HOURS LATER, HE FALLS INTO A DEEP SLEEP. BEING IN HIS OWN BED BRINGS A CERTAIN COMFORT: THE SECURITY TO RELAX.
AND DREAM ABOUT PEOPLE AND THINGS.
THINGS HAUNTING.
THINGS FAMILIAR.
AL.
THE DREAM REPEATS ITSELF, OVER AND OVER.

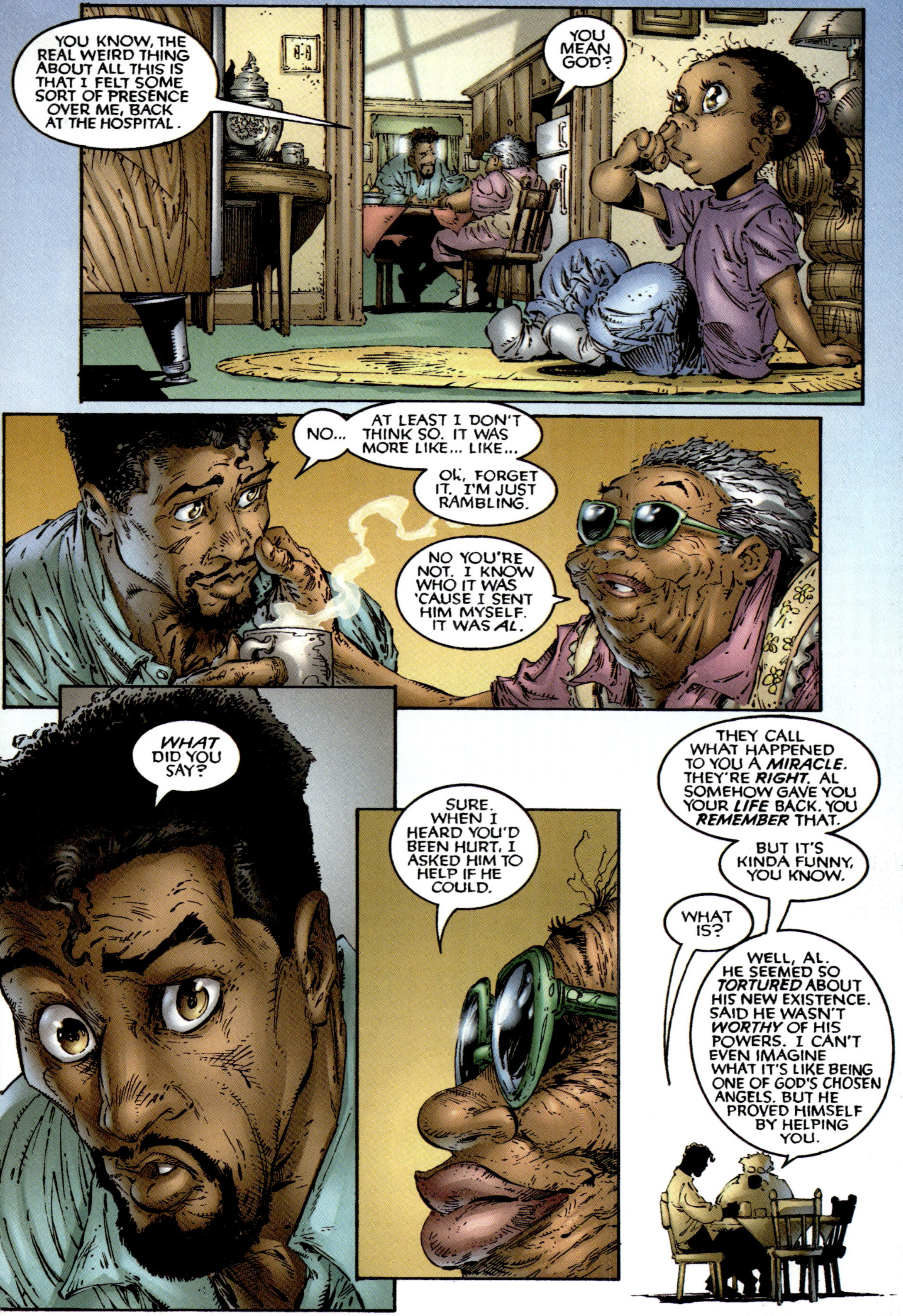

YOU KNOW, THE REAL WEIRD THING ABOUT ALL THIS IS THAT I FELT SOME SORT OF PRESENCE OVER ME, BACK AT THE HOSPITAL.
YOU MEAN GOD?
NO... AT LEAST I DON'T THINK SO. IT WAS MORE LIKE... LIKE...
OH, FORGET IT. I'M JUST RAMBLING.
NO YOU'RE NOT. I KNOW WHO IT WAS 'CAUSE I SENT HIM MYSELF. IT WAS AL.
WHAT DID YOU SAY?
SURE. WHEN I HEARD YOU'D BEEN HURT, I ASKED HIM TO HELP IF HE COULD.
THEY CALL WHAT HAPPENED TO YOU A MIRACLE. THEY'RE RIGHT. AL SOMEHOW GAVE YOU YOUR LIFE BACK. YOU REMEMBER THAT.
BUT IT'S KINDA FUNNY, YOU KNOW.
WHAT IS?
WELL, AL. HE SEEMED SO TORTURED ABOUT HIS NEW EXISTENCE. SAID HE WASN'T WORTHY OF HIS POWERS. I CAN'T EVEN IMAGINE WHAT IT'S LIKE BEING ONE OF GOD'S CHOSEN ANGELS. BUT HE PROVED HIMSELF BY HELPING YOU.

WITH ALL CONCEPT OF TIME OBLITERATED, SPAWN'S ETHEREAL PRESENCE BREAKS THE BLACK VEIL.
A YEAR? A DAY? A SECOND?
NO ONE KNOWS HOW MUCH TIME THE SOUL'S TRANSITION TAKES, BUT DEATH MAKES IT INEVITABLE.
AT THAT POINT, THERE IS ONE RULE ADHERED TO BY BOTH SIDES:
"THOSE SOULS WHO SHALL RETURN TO THE AFTERLIFE PAST THE INITIAL ENTRY WILL FOREVER BE REMANDED TO THEIR FIRST LORD."
IN SHORT, SPAWN HAS RETURNED TO HELL.

TO COMPLETE THE ODYSSEY, HIS SPIRIT NESTLES ONCE MORE INTO THE FORM IT INHABITED MOST RECENTLY.
THOUGH HE DOESN'T RECALL THE EVENTS FOLLOWING HIS FIRST DEATH, WHAT HE SEES APPEARS UNFAMILIAR.
IT IS.
STRETCHED NOW BEFORE HIM IS A VAST WASTELAND: HELL'S SECOND LEVEL.
AS A FORMER VISITOR TO ANOTHER, HIGHER LEVEL, HIS PRESENCE IS ACKNOWLEDGED IMMEDIATELY:
AN ENEMY HAS TRESPASSED IN THEIR SACRED LANDS.

THEY APPEAR OUT OF NOWHERE... GNATS... THAT GAPING WOUND IN HIS FACE, NO LONGER TIED SHUT, ALLOWS THEM TO DIG DEEPLY.
WHILE HE'S DISTRACTED, THE GROUND ITSELF JOINS THE FRAY, SWALLOWING ONE LEG AND HOLDING IT IN A DEATH GRIP.
IT'S ONLY THE START.
NEK-TORR
ANOTHER WAVE CONVERGES, SCREAMING PAST THE CLOAKED HERO. SUDDENLY, THEY SNATCH A FEW OF HIS CAPE'S TENDRILS.
THEIR ATTACK IS FAR FROM RANDOM, HE REALIZES.
THEN, BURROWING UNDERGROUND, THE LEATHERY CREATURES DISAPPEAR.
THE HELLSPAWN IS NOW PULLED TAUT AS A STAKED TENT.

INTRUDERS WILL NOT BE PERMITTED-- EVEN THOSE FROM OTHER LEVELS.
NEK-TORR
NEK-TORR
NEK-TORR
NEK-TORR
NEK-TORR
THE UNHOLY LAWS REQUIRE THE STRAINS REMAIN PURE.
HYBRIDS WILL ONLY DESTROY THEIR UTOPIA.
YET, WITHOUT THE HYBRIDS, THEY CANNOT LIVE.
AND SO, INTRUDERS THAT HAVE TRIED TO CROSS THE VOID INTO THE NEXT LEVEL ARE PUT TO A PURPOSE BEFORE THEY DIE THE DEATH OF HELL.
NEK-TORR
NEK-TORR

INSANITY SPIRALLING AROUND HIM, SPAWN TRIES TO KEEP A GRIP, EVEN AS THE WEIGHT OF THE DEMON HORDE PREPARES TO SUFFOCATE HIM.
NEK-TORR
THROUGH THE CRACKS, THE SMALL ONES GET THERE FIRST.
AS HIS VISION BEGINS TO BLUR, AL SIMMONS WONDERS WHAT HE DID TO DESERVE THIS FATE -- THIS CURSE OF THE SPAWN.
NEK-TORR
THEY ARE NOWHERE. THEY ARE EVERYWHERE.
FIGHTING EACH OTHER FOR POSITION.
WAS IT THE KILLINGS?
HE WAS ONLY FOLLOWING ORDERS, HE THINKS.
TOTAL DAMNATION FOR ANY MURDERER, THAT'S WHAT IT MUST BE.
SO HE GIVES IN AND GOES LIMP, JUST AS THE PARCHED LAND GOES BLACK.
NEK-TORR?!

BUT HELL, LIKE HEAVEN, WAS NEVER MEANT FOR MAN TO UNDERSTAND.
IT'S A PLACE OF PAIN. HORROR. ANGUISH. FAR BEYOND ANYTHING POSSIBLE ON EARTH.
NEK-TORR MEFEE!
YET, AS ON EARTH, A PECKING ORDER HAS EVOLVED-- ONE PREDICATED ON SIZE. NOT SURPRISINGLY, RESENTMENT EXISTS.
A PILLAR OF THEIR REMAINS PETRIFIES IN A HEART-BEAT...
THEY FOUND HIM FIRST, THE SMALL ONES DID.
THEY'LL NOT LEAVE HIM BEHIND.
NEK-TORR!
...LEAVING JUST AN EXPOSED TIP.

NOW FULLY EXPOSED FOR THE TAKING, SPAWN'S HEAD WAS THE ULTIMATE PRIZE ... THOUGH NOT HIM AS MUCH AS WHAT MADE HIM:

NECROPLASM. CONCOCTED AN INFINITY AGO IN HELL'S DARKEST REACHES, IT SERVES MANY USES ON MANY LEVELS.

IN MALEBOLGIA'S REALM, IT'S WHAT HIS WARRIORS ARE MADE OF.

BUT HERE, THE PLASM HAS ANOTHER PURPOSE: FOOD. WITHOUT TRESPASSERS TO FEAST ON, THE INHABITANTS WOULD HAVE PERISHED LONG AGO.

SO, EACH VICTIM BECAME THEIR VITAL NOURISHMENT.

THEIR CALORIES. THEIR JUICES.

THEIR SWEET NECTAR.

SPAWN WILL HAVE NONE OF IT. IF HE IS TO DIE HERE, THEN HE MEANS TO TAKE AS MANY OF THEM WITH HIM AS POSSIBLE.
HE THOUGHT HE'D JUST GIVE UP AND DIE. HE CHANGED HIS MIND.
LT. COLONEL AL SIMMONS HAS ONE MORE FIGHT LEFT IN HIM.
GREEN ENERGY CRACKLES. SINCE HE'S A PRISONER OF HELL, WHAT DOES SPAWN CARE ABOUT CONSERVING HIS POWERS ANY LONGER?
FOR A HUNDRED MILES THE SKIES TURN GREEN.
IT'S HIS WAY OF EXORCIZING HIS OWN PERSONAL DEMONS.
HIS WIFE IS LOST TO HIM. FOREVER.
SHEER ANGER IS ALL THAT COMES FROM THAT THOUGHT.

PREPARE, DEMON, TO EAT YOUR HEART!
ADRENALINE IS TRIGGERED.
RELEASING ONCE AGAIN THE TRUE SPIRIT OF THE WARRIOR.
BRACED AGAINST PETRIFIED DEBRIS, HE STANDS READY FOR ATTACK.

FOOD. THAT'S ALL SPAWN IS TO THE CHARGING MONSTROSITY.
SOMETHING TO FEED ITS CRAVINGS. NO MATTER THE SOURCE.
ITS OWN SLAVES OFTEN FILL THE BILL.
IF YOU'RE SO GODDAMNED HUNGRY...
...CHOKE ON THIS!
LIKE SOME CRAZED TARZAN, SPAWN CLIMBS ATOP HIS KILL. FROTHING AT THE MOUTH, HE LETS RIP A NOISE NO HUMAN COULD POSSIBLY CONCEIVE OF.
THE SOUND, AUDIBLE OUT TO THE DESERT, IS CUT SHORT WHEN THE HELLSPAWN ABRUPTLY EVAPORATES.

ELSEWHERE IN TIME...
Perfect!
It went just as I'd planned. My little Spawn has just picked up the first of his new gifts.
Unknowingly, of course.
A few more pieces and my 'Grim Reaper' will be ready. Enjoy your next level, Simmons.
C'MON, HONEY! TIME TO GO HOME. THANK MEGAN FOR INVITING YOU TO HER PARTY.
BALLOON! BALLOON!
OKAY, GO GRAB ONE.
THERE YOU ARE, DEAR, SWEET CYAN.
YOU'RE FUNNY.
THANK YOU.
BYE-BYE. I'LL SEE YOU SOON.
Hee hee hee hee hee

image
SPAWN
51
JUL
$1.95
$3.75 Canada

FRAGMENTED INTO A THOUSAND SECTIONS SPREAD ALL ACROSS THE NINE LEVELS, THE CATACOMBS OF HELL OFFER EVERY VARIANT OF MACABRE SCENERY IMAGINABLE.

THIS IS ONE SUCH SLIVER.

IT HAS BEEN CALLED BY MANY NAMES, THIS NIGHTMARE PLACE, AND YET IT REMAINS NAMELESS, OWING TO THE LIMITS OF THE HUMAN TONGUE, THE FRAGILITY OF THE HUMAN MIND.

AND IN SOME DARK, VILE CORNER OF SATAN'S PLAY-GROUND, THE DAMNED WHISPER OF WHAT IS POSSIBLY THE HARSHEST LEVEL OF ALL:

THE FOURTH.

EARTH'S CURRENT HELLSPAWN IS ABOUT TO BECOME ITS NEWEST VICTIM.

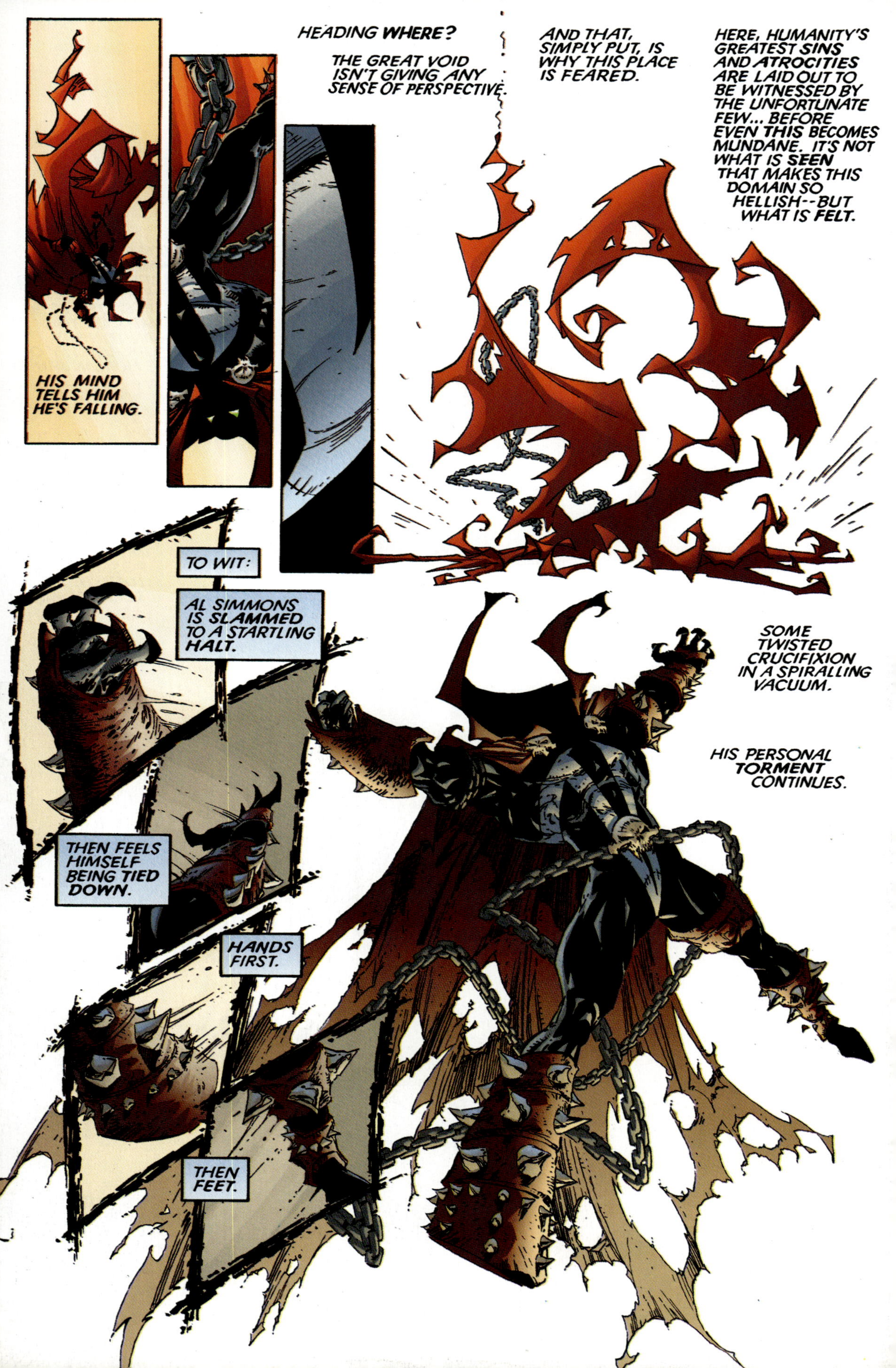

HEADING WHERE?
THE GREAT VOID ISN'T GIVING ANY SENSE OF PERSPECTIVE.
AND THAT, SIMPLY PUT, IS WHY THIS PLACE IS FEARED.
HERE, HUMANITY'S GREATEST SINS AND ATROCITIES ARE LAID OUT TO BE WITNESSED BY THE UNFORTUNATE FEW... BEFORE EVEN THIS BECOMES MUNDANE. IT'S NOT WHAT IS SEEN THAT MAKES THIS DOMAIN SO HELLISH--BUT WHAT IS FELT.
HIS MIND TELLS HIM HE'S FALLING.
SOME TWISTED CRUCIFIXION IN A SPIRALLING VACUUM.
HIS PERSONAL TORMENT CONTINUES.
TO WIT:
AL SIMMONS IS SLAMMED TO A STARTLING HALT.
THEN FEELS HIMSELF BEING TIED DOWN.
HANDS FIRST.
THEN FEET.

STRUGGLE AS HE MAY, HIS INVISIBLE BONDS HOLD FAST.
WHATEVER HE HIT-- WHATEVER PINS HIM-- FEELS TANGIBLE. FORMIDABLE.
HIS EYES TELL HIM OTHERWISE.
WHAT KIND OF MADNESS IS THIS?
A PRIVATE ONE. SAVED EXCLUSIVELY FOR HIM.
THEN, THE NOISE: HIS FIRST CLUE. AND THE SECOND: PAIN.
IT GROWS SHARPER AS THE SYMBIOTIC COSTUME, ATTACHED TO HIS NECROPLASMIC NERVES, BEGINS TO PEEL ITSELF FROM ITS HOST.
EEIIAA
DETACHMENT. HE'S BEEN THROUGH IT ONCE BEFORE, ON EARTH.
HE PRAYED HE'D NEVER HAVE TO LIVE THROUGH THAT AGAIN. UNFORTUNATELY, PLEADING FOR GOD'S MERCY ISN'T PERMITTED HERE.

NOT IN ANY SHAPE OR FORM.
BUT OTHERS ARE GLAD FOR THE ENTERTAINMENT-- SUCH AS THE LATEST UNHOLY RULER OF THIS TERRITORY.
AWWWH... THERE YOU ARE!

GOOD. THEY SAID YOU WERE WAITING. SORRY FOR THE DELAY. I WAS JUST FINISHING UP SOME LAST-MINUTE SEWING.
NOW... SIMMONS IS YOUR NAME, I BELIEVE... IS THAT RIGHT?

SCREW YOU!
SPIRITED. THAT WAS ON YOUR RESUME.
THIS SHOULD BE A FUN SESSION.

YOU KNOW, IT'S NOT OFTEN WE GET TO DEAL WITH ONE OF MALEBOLGIA'S ELITE.
I THINK IT'S BEEN A COUPLE MILLENNIA SINCE THE LAST. BUT, WE'RE HERE FOR YOU, AREN'T WE?
NOW, WHERE WOULD YOU LIKE TO START? YOUR CHILDHOOD, PERHAPS?

MY CHILDHOOD?!
YOU'RE RIGHT. NOTHING TOO DYSFUNCTIONAL IN THAT AREA. IT WAS A GOOD ENVIRONMENT.
WHAT DO YOU WANT FROM ME?
THE SAME THING YOU WANT. ANSWERS.
TO WHAT?!! YOU'VE ALREADY WON. HELL HAS ME.
BUT YOU DIDN'T COME WILLINGLY.
THAT'S THE KEY. YOU SEE, ONLY WHEN YOU'VE ACCEPTED WHAT YOU ARE WILL YOU EVER BE AT PEACE. EMBRACE THE EVIL THAT LIVES INSIDE. IT'S PART OF YOU-- JUST LIKE ALL THIS AROUND YOU.
HUH?
I DON'T CARE ABOUT YOUR FRIGGIN' HALLUCINATIONS.
HOW DARE YOU?!!
WHAT'S HERE IS REAL. VERY REAL. AND IT ALL COMES FROM YOU: THE HUMANS. YOUR CAPACITY FOR EVIL CREATED THESE HORRIFIC CONDITIONS THAT ARE RECREATED HERE. BUT WHAT'S OF FAR GREATER IMPORTANCE IS WHERE THE ACTS ARE BORN:
THE SINS OF MAN. THEY'RE HERE. I CAN SEE THEM. A MUGGING OVER THERE, SOME RAPING, CHEATING AND ABUSE IN THAT CORNER... IT'S QUITE LOVELY.

IT'S THE SOUL.
YOU CAN'T SEE IT, YET IT'S FELT BY ALL. THAT'S WHAT THIS PLACE IS-- A HOLDING TANK FOR DARK EMOTIONS.
THE ACTUAL PHYSICAL STUFF I LEAVE TO THE OTHER KINGDOMS. HERE, WE GET TO THE CORE OF PROBLEMS BY STRIPPING AWAY ALL THE BARNACLES.
SO THE EASY QUESTION IS, WHY ARE YOU HERE?
WANDA.
NOT QUITE. YES, IT DOES HAVE SOMETHING TO DO WITH LOVE, BUT NOT THE KIND YOU'RE THINKING OF.
IT'S DOWN TO YOUR LOVE OF KILLING.
YOU'RE WRONG.
GYAAAA
REALLY?
THEN YOUR MIND'S BEEN CLOUDED. LET'S PULL THAT LAYER AWAY AND RECONSTRUCT A FEW MOMENTS FROM YOUR PAST.

YOUR FIRST KILL. DO YOU REMEMBER HIS FACE?

THAT WAS AN EASY ONE, WASN'T IT? BUT AS TIME MOVED ON, THE HABIT BECAME ENTRENCHED. YOUR DESIRE FOR MAYHEM DIDN'T NEED MUCH MOTIVATING.

SOON, INNOCENTS WERE CAUGHT IN THE CROSSFIRE. ALL THE WHILE, YOU FELT ABSOLVED BECAUSE, AS A GOOD SOLDIER, YOU WERE FOLLOWING ORDERS.

THEY DECORATED YOU MANY TIMES, FOR HEROISM.

IT FELT GOOD, DIDN'T IT?

UNFORTUNATELY, YOU WERE TOO SKILLED. SO, AS YOUR ASSIGNMENTS BECAME BLOODIER, YOUR VALUE INCREASED EXPONENTIALLY HERE IN HELL.

YOUR SPECIAL KIND OF LOVE IS VERY RARE INDEED.

THEY'VE BEEN HEMMING AND HAWING FOR CLOSE TO AN HOUR NOW, THREE SPECIALISTS TRYING TO SOLVE ANOTHER MEDICAL MYSTERY...
HOW'RE YOU HOLDING UP, TERRY?
JUST PEACHY.
BUNCHA QUACKS.
AN INTERESTING THEORY, Dr. ROLLINS, THOUGH IT DOESN'T TAKE INTO ACCOUNT HIS FAIRLY UNREMARKABLE GENETIC MAKEUP.
YES. WELL, SINCE THIS PHENOMENON HAS ONLY BEEN DOCUMENTED IN CONNECTION WITH THE GOVERNMENT'S SUPER-HUMANS, PERHAPS OUR PATIENT ISN'T WHAT HE APPEARS.
MY FEELINGS EXACTLY. MUCH AS WE'D LIKE TO QUANTIFY THIS MIRACULOUS RECOVERY, IT'S DIFFICULT TO KNOW HOW TO FRAME THE QUESTIONS. Mr. FITZGERALD, ARE YOU CERTAIN THAT ALL THE DATA WE HAVE IS CORRECT?
YUP.

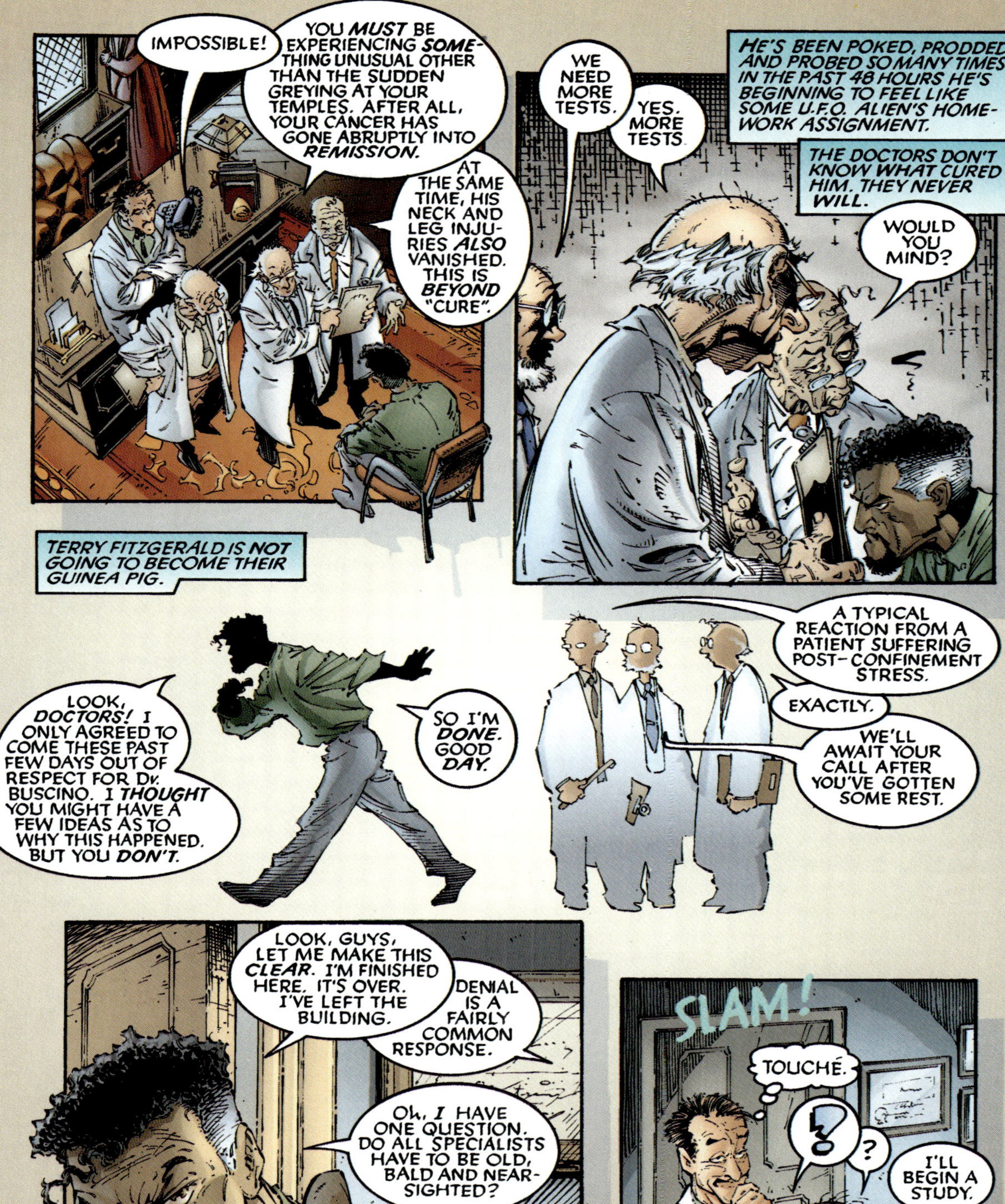

IMPOSSIBLE!

YOU *MUST* BE EXPERIENCING *SOME-*THING UNUSUAL OTHER THAN THE SUDDEN GREYING AT YOUR TEMPLES. AFTER ALL, YOUR CANCER HAS GONE ABRUPTLY INTO *REMISSION.*

AT THE SAME TIME, HIS NECK AND LEG INJU-RIES *ALSO* VANISHED. THIS IS *BEYOND* "CURE".

WE NEED MORE TESTS.

YES, MORE TESTS.

HE'S BEEN POKED, PRODDED AND PROBED SO MANY TIMES IN THE PAST 48 HOURS HE'S BEGINNING TO FEEL LIKE SOME U.F.O. ALIEN'S HOME-WORK ASSIGNMENT.

THE DOCTORS DON'T KNOW WHAT CURED HIM. THEY NEVER WILL.

WOULD YOU MIND?

TERRY FITZGERALD IS *NOT* GOING TO BECOME THEIR GUINEA PIG.

LOOK, *DOCTORS!* I ONLY AGREED TO COME THESE PAST FEW DAYS OUT OF RESPECT FOR Dr. BUSCINO. I *THOUGHT* YOU MIGHT HAVE A FEW IDEAS AS TO WHY THIS HAPPENED. BUT YOU *DON'T.*

SO I'M *DONE.* GOOD *DAY.*

A TYPICAL REACTION FROM A PATIENT SUFFERING POST—CONFINEMENT STRESS.

EXACTLY.

WE'LL AWAIT YOUR CALL AFTER YOU'VE GOTTEN SOME REST.

LOOK, GUYS, LET ME MAKE THIS *CLEAR.* I'M FINISHED HERE. IT'S OVER. I'VE LEFT THE BUILDING.

DENIAL IS A FAIRLY COMMON RESPONSE.

OH, I HAVE ONE QUESTION. DO ALL SPECIALISTS HAVE TO BE OLD, BALD AND NEAR-SIGHTED?

SLAM!

TOUCHÉ.

?

I'LL BEGIN A STUDY.

C'MON, TERRY. THEY WEREN'T THAT BAD.
OH YEAH?! I THOUGHT I'D BE A LITTLE MORE COMPASSION-ATE AFTER MY NEAR-DEATH, BUT THOSE GUYS DROVE ME CRAZY.
THE WAY THEY TALK--! IT ISN'T NORMAL. BESIDES, I DON'T TRUST ANYONE THAT USES WORDS BIGGER THAN 'BANANA'.
THEY'RE JUST DOING THEIR JOB. IT'S TOO BAD THEY COULDN'T SHED ANY LIGHT ON YOUR RECOVERY.
YOU SEEM PERFECTLY HEALTHY BUT A PART OF ME IS STILL HAVING A HARD TIME DEALING WITH ALL THIS.

YOU'VE ALREADY HEARD MY OPINION.
NOT THAT WHOLE 'SEXUAL TENSION' THING AGAIN--!
ONLY WHEN I'M AWAKE OR ASLEEP. THAT'S IT.
IS THAT ALL YOU THINK ABOUT?

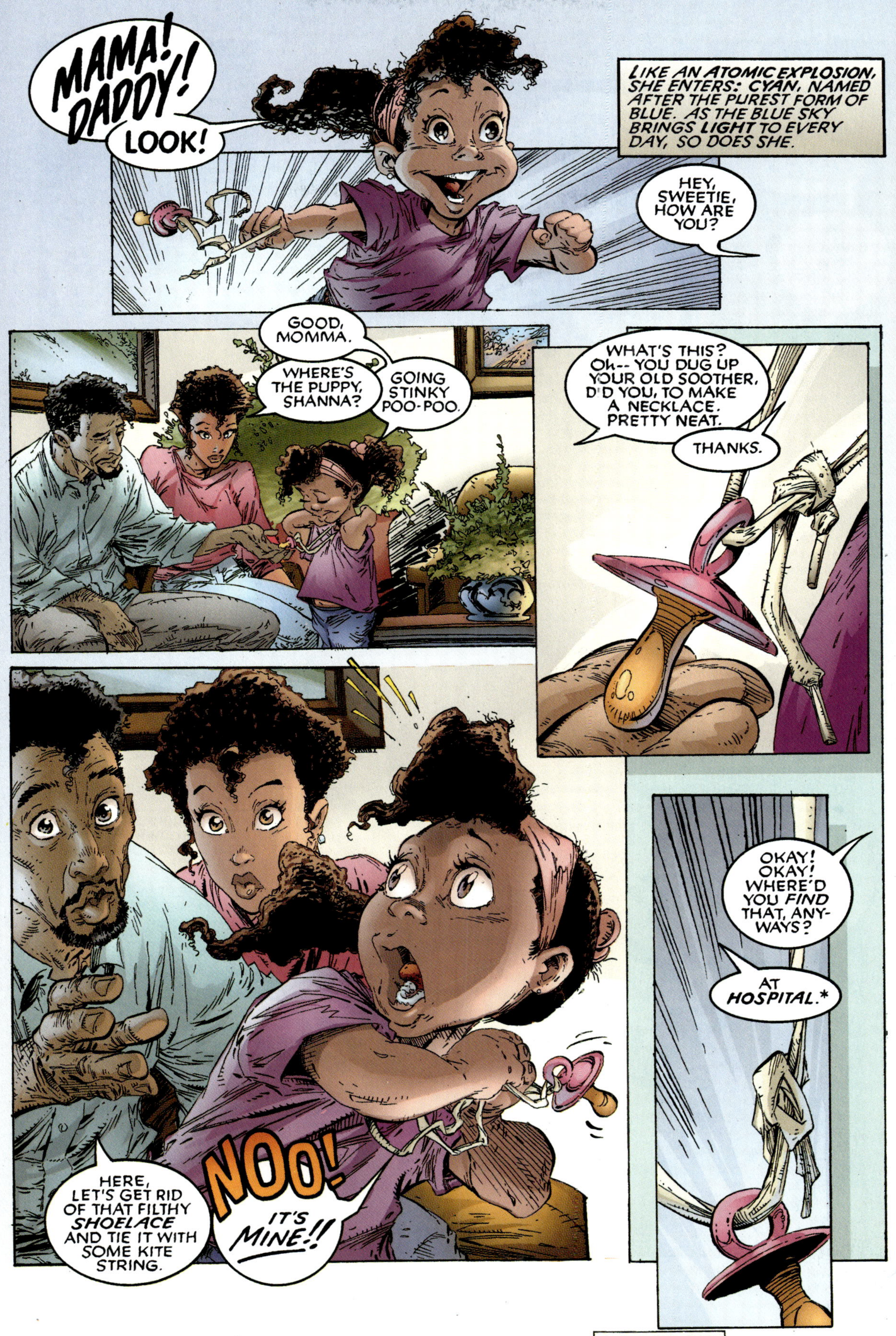

MAMA! DADDY! LOOK!
LIKE AN ATOMIC EXPLOSION, SHE ENTERS: CYAN, NAMED AFTER THE PUREST FORM OF BLUE. AS THE BLUE SKY BRINGS LIGHT TO EVERY DAY, SO DOES SHE.
HEY, SWEETIE, HOW ARE YOU?
GOOD, MOMMA.
WHERE'S THE PUPPY, SHANNA?
GOING STINKY POO-POO.
WHAT'S THIS? OH-- YOU DUG UP YOUR OLD SOOTHER, D'D YOU, TO MAKE A NECKLACE. PRETTY NEAT.
THANKS.
OKAY! OKAY! WHERE'D YOU FIND THAT, ANY-WAYS?
AT HOSPITAL.*
HERE, LET'S GET RID OF THAT FILTHY SHOELACE AND TIE IT WITH SOME KITE STRING.
NOO! IT'S MINE!!
*LAST ISSUE -- Tom.

CRIPES!
THIS IS GIVING ME A BLEEDING ULCER.
NOW EXPLAIN TO ME, AGAIN, WHY WE NEED TO BE CONCERNED ABOUT THIS SNITCH, ESPECIALLY AFTER HE STOOD US UP FOR OUR FIRST MEETING. WHO NEEDS HIM?
IT'S THE PAYING CLIENTS THAT INTEREST ME.
WE NEED HIM BECAUSE HE KNOWS THINGS, SIR.
THINGS HE SHOULDN'T.
FOR INSTANCE?
OH, HEY-- YA NEED SOME PIZZA?
NO THANKS
TAKE A LOOK AT THIS. IT'S A DETAILED RUN-DOWN OF EVERY BANK ACCOUNT CONTROLLED BY SENATOR JENNINGS' CAMPAIGN. IT LISTS DOMESTIC AS WELL AS INTERNATIONAL HOLDINGS.
SO OUR 'DEEP THROAT' IS SOME GOVERN-MENT STIFF. WHAT'S THE SURPRISE?
LOOK HOW IT WORKS THROUGH. CHIEF BANKS BLOWS HIS HEAD OFF. THEN, EVEN THOUGH WE GAVE PLENTY OF DAMAGING EVIDENCE TO THE PAPERS, EVERY-THING GETS SWEPT UNDER THE CARPET, LEAVING BANKS HANGING THERE, ALL BY HIMSELF.
SO WHY IS THERE ALSO SUCH A FOCUS ON SENATOR JENNINGS? HE RETIRED YEARS AGO. IT SUGGESTS SOMEONE BIGGER IS PULLING THE STRINGS... AS WE SUSPECTED.
*ISSUE 43--Tom.

MEANING-- EITHER OUR MYSTERY MAN IS SOME CRACKPOT--
--OR--
--WE'VE GOT OURSELVES A VERY HIGH PROFILE INFORMANT.
WHO'S LOOKING TO BRING DOWN SOMEONE, SERIOUS.
OKAY, SO WE HANG WITH THIS GUY A LITTLE LONGER. I'M STILL CURIOUS ABOUT HOW HE FOUND US SO QUICKLY.
AND HOW THE HELL DID HE GET OUR PHONE NUMBER THE DAY IT WAS INSTALLED?
WE'LL FIND OUT WEDNESDAY.
SERAFINI'S PIZZA
PBLLLT!
AW, COME ON, TWITCH! IT WAS JUST A LITTLE FART. BESIDES, I KINDA LIKE THE WAY IT SMELLS.
sniff
SNIF SNIF
OHMYGOD!!!
OHMYGOD!
OHMYGOD!
SNIFFFFF
ahhh...
AIR!!
YOU GONNA LIVE?
I'D APPRECIATE A LITTLE CONSIDERATION NEXT TIME, SIR! EVEN HITLER GAVE A WARNING BEFORE HE ATTACKED!
DETECTIVE WILLIAMS NOTICES SOMETHING BELOW.
SIR, GRAB YOUR GUN, NOW!

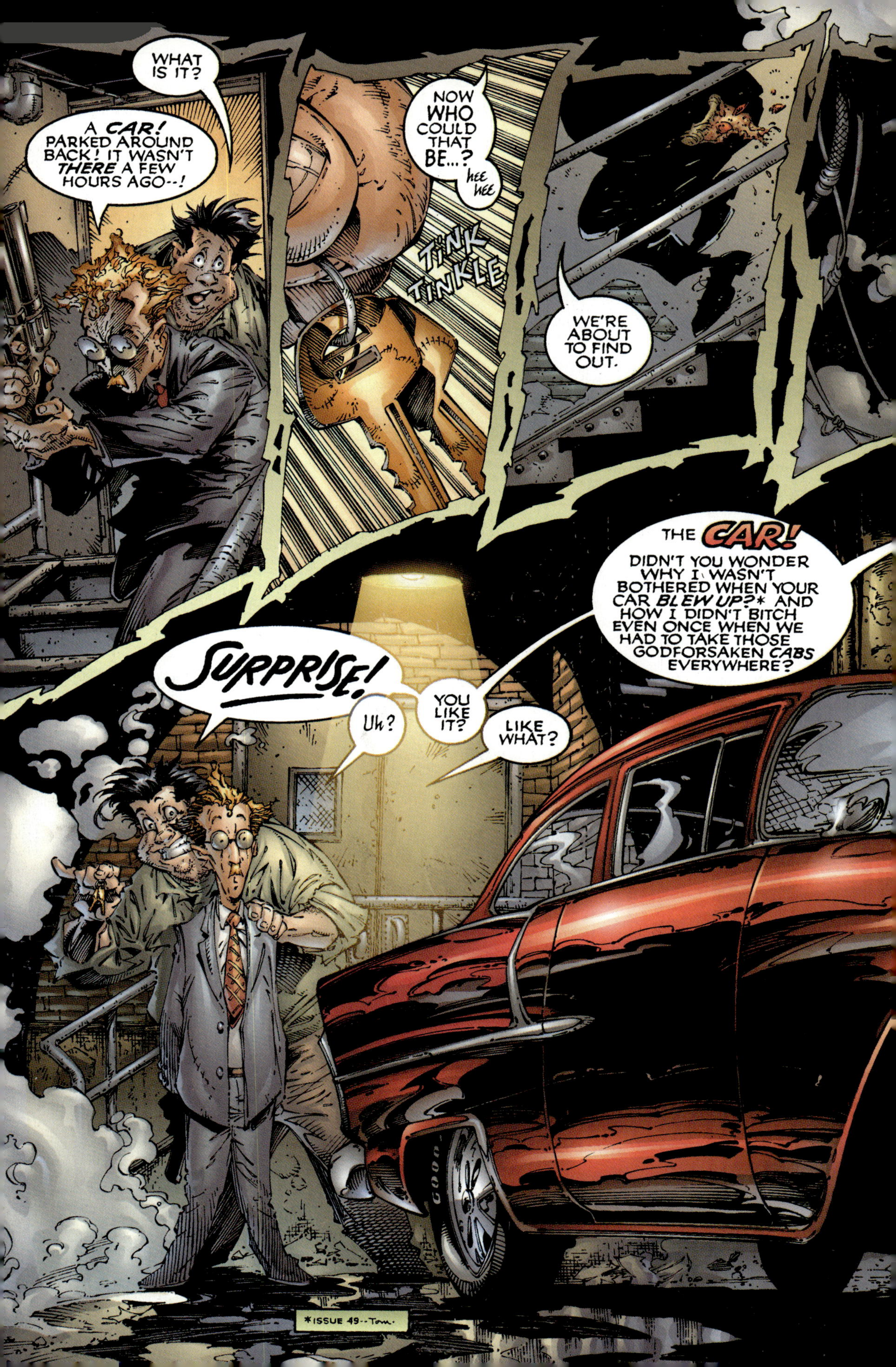

WHAT IS IT?
A CAR! PARKED AROUND BACK! IT WASN'T THERE A FEW HOURS AGO--!
NOW WHO COULD THAT BE...?
HEE HEE
TINK TINKLE
WE'RE ABOUT TO FIND OUT.
THE CAR! DIDN'T YOU WONDER WHY I WASN'T BOTHERED WHEN YOUR CAR BLEW UP?* AND HOW I DIDN'T BITCH EVEN ONCE WHEN WE HAD TO TAKE THOSE GODFORSAKEN CABS EVERYWHERE?
SURPRISE!
UH?
YOU LIKE IT?
LIKE WHAT?
*ISSUE 49--Tom.

BAM
...FINDING NO ONE.
ITH THE RACTICED UTION OF FIFTEEN-AR VET, ITCH EEPS THE LEY IN BEAT...
WHAT KIND OF IDIOT WOULD PARK THAT AROUND HERE?!
NOPE!
I THOUGHT YOU WERE MATURING.
IT WAS 'CAUSE I KNEW THIS WAS COMING. AIN'T IT A BEAUTY? A '55 CHEVY. COMPLETELY REBUILT FOR HIGH PERFORMANCE. I KEPT PART OF MY RESERVE CASH TO GET THIS.
I ALWAYS DREAMED OF ONE OF THESE BABIES, BUT NEVER HAD A GOOD ENOUGH REASON TO BUY ONE UNTIL NOW. IF WE'RE GOING TO BE A LEGITIMATE DETECTIVE AGENCY THEN WE OUGHT TO LOOK THE PART.
I CALL IT The CRIMEMOBILE. WHADDAYA THINK?
IT IS IMPRESSIVE, SIR.
THANKS. AND, um, SORRY ABOUT THOSE BEER-AND-PIZZA FARTS.

SO, WE'VE VENTURED THROUGH YOUR FIRST EMOTIONAL BARRIER. I KNOW, IT'S QUITE PAINFUL TO HEAR THE TRUTH. BUT LUCKILY, MOST OF YOU HUMANS HAVE ONLY A COUPLE OF BIG FLAWS TO WORK THROUGH.
SO, LET US PROCEED.
WE'VE SEEN YOUR LUST FOR KILLING. SO, WHAT ELSE HAVE YOU GOT?
HOW ABOUT HATE? OH, YOU'VE A GIANT RESERVOIR FOR THAT. TAKE JASON WYNN, FOR EXAMPLE. WHILE HE WAS YOUR BOSS, HE CONTROLLED MOST EVERY FACET OF YOUR "BUSINESS" CAREER.
SOON, THAT CONTROL GREW MORE EXACTING, LEADING TO TENSION. ARGUMENTS. ANGER.
EVENTUALLY, HE FOUND IT NECESSARY TO HAVE YOU MURDERED.
SENDING YOU TO US.

YOU LOVED THAT, DIDN'T YOU. TO HATE HIM, I MEAN. YOU HATED HIM WHEN YOU WERE ALIVE, AND YOUR DEATH GAVE YOU NO REASON TO CHANGE YOUR MIND.
YOU SHOULD BE PROUD.
MALEBOLGIA IS. HATEFUL KILLERS RATE HIGH ON HIS LIST.
AND THOSE WITH SPECIAL APTITUDE-- LIKE YOURSELF-- GET A BONUS.
THE COSTUME.
BY NOW, I'M SURE YOU'VE BEEN WONDERING WHAT'S HAPPENED TO IT-- WHY IT'S NOT PROTECTING YOU. QUITE SIMPLE. IT'S HOME.
WE GROW THEM HERE, YOU SEE. WHEN THEY'RE FULLY FUNCTIONAL, WE DELIVER THEM TO MALEBOLGIA'S EIGHTH LEVEL FOR ATTACHMENT.
FROM AMONG THEM, ONLY A SELECT FEW GET TO GRAFT TO HIS CHOSEN OFFICERS.
WE'RE SO HAPPY FOR THIS K-125 UNIT.

HE'S BEEN DOWN AT YOUR FEET ALL THIS TIME. THEY CAN BE A RATHER SHY LOT AROUND THEIR MAKERS.
YOU'VE BECOME A HELLSPAWN, NOT SO MUCH BECAUSE YOU ARE EVIL, BUT IN ANTICIPATION OF THE REALIZATION OF YOUR FULL POTENTIAL.
THAT'S HOW SOULS REACH HEAVEN OR HELL.
BUT I DIGRESS.
YOU, MR. SIMMONS, ARE NO DIFFERENT.
BUT YOU HAVEN'T ACCEPTED THAT.
WHY?
BECAUSE OF WANDA.
AND YOUR SUPPOSED LOVE FOR HER.
AIEEE

PLEASE, EXCUSE THE PAIN. THOSE WHO'VE PRECEEDED YOU BEGGED FOR THEIR OWN PHYSICALITY HERE, SINCE NOTHING TANGIBLE WAS AROUND TO ASSURE THEM THEY STILL EXISTED.
SO I SKINNED THEM.
THEN I SEWED THEIR FORMS TO MY OWN·· A SOUVENIR OF OUR TIME TOGETHER.
AFTER ALL, WE NEED TO BE REMINDED OF THE PAST. OF TIME LOST.
REMEMBER THE FIRST TIME YOU SAW HER...? IT TOOK YOU NEARLY FOUR DAYS TO GET UP THE NERVE TO INTRODUCE YOURSELF.
AND AFTER ALL THAT, ON YOUR FIRST FEW DATES SHE DIDN'T EVEN SEEM PARTICULARLY INTERESTED.
BEFORE LONG, THAT CHANGED. YOUR COURTSHIP, THE GIVE-AND-TAKE, SHOWED THE SYMPATHIES YOU BOTH EMBRACED.
THEN, IN ALMOST NO TIME, A FULL-BLOWN LOVE SPROUTED IN YOU BOTH. YOU GOT YOUR WISH, THAT YOU'D SPEND THE REST OF YOUR LIVES TOGETHER.

IT ALL SEEMED SO PERFECT, DIDN'T IT? SO WHAT IF YOU COULDN'T FATHER ANY CHILDREN. SO WHAT IF YOUR SECRET ASSIGNMENTS TOOK YOU AWAY FOR WEEKS AT A TIME? LOVE WOULD CARRY YOU.
YOUR LOVE FOR BLOOD. YOUR LOVE FOR WANDA.
THEY EXPANDED SIMULTANEOUSLY.
ONE FOUGHT THE OTHER FOR PRIMACY. BECAUSE LOVE, AL, NEEDS A CONSTANT FLOW OF NOURISHMENT. SOMETHING HAD TO GIVE.
SURPRISE! IT WAS YOU.
AT FIRST, WANDA MOURNED. HER HEART ACHED. A LOVING WIFE GOES THROUGH THAT.
SHE ALSO LOVED YOU SO MUCH THAT SHE THEN FOUND COMFORT IN ANOTHER MAN. YOUR FRIEND. AND, WELL, HIS PLUMBING WORKED. THEIR DAUGHTER ALMOST MADE THEM FORGET YOU.
WHAT DID THEY CARE ABOUT YOU, AFTER ALL? THEY HAD EACH OTHER. TO CHERISH. TO LUST AFTER. TO LOVE!

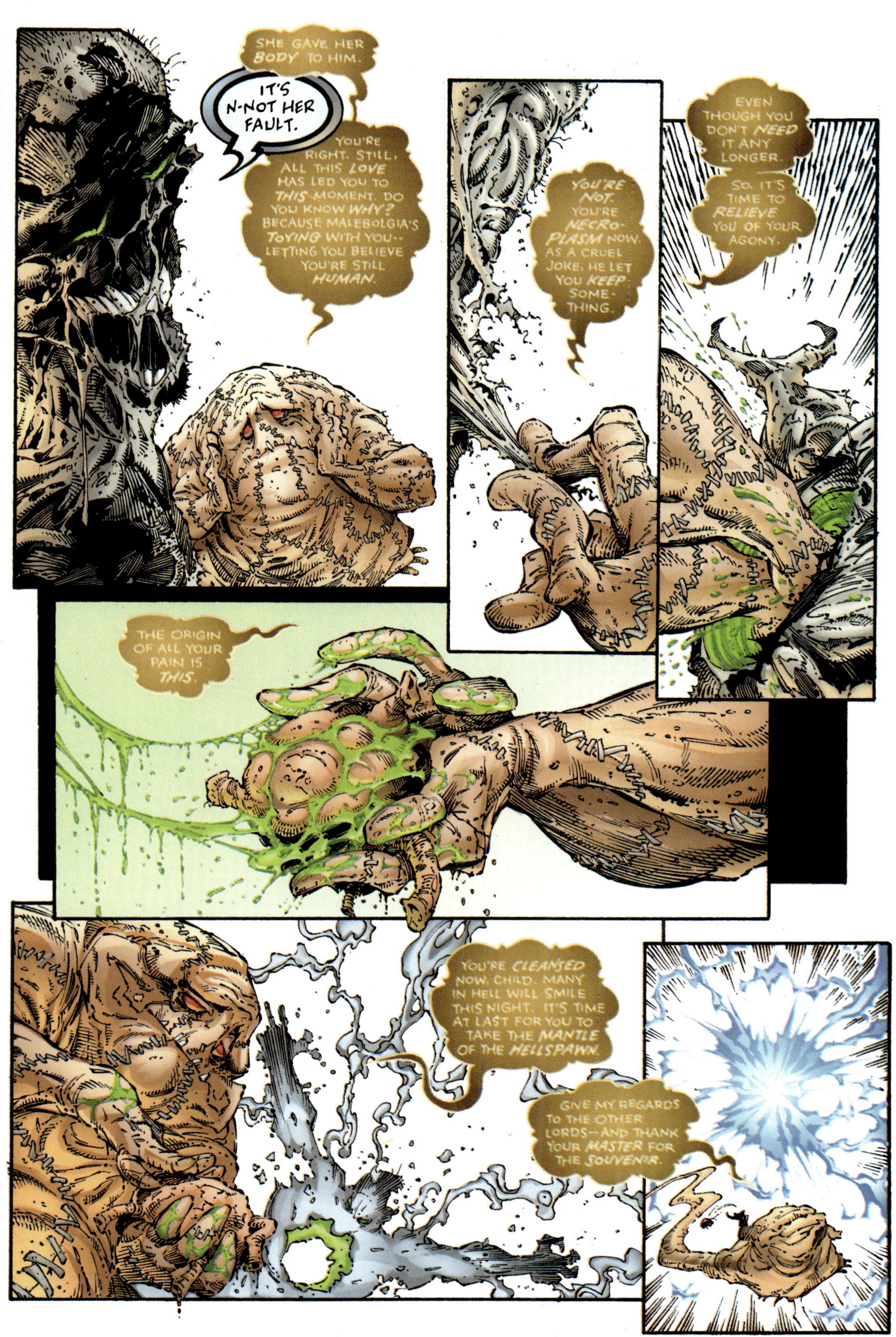

SHE GAVE HER BODY TO HIM.
IT'S N-NOT HER FAULT.
YOU'RE RIGHT. STILL, ALL THIS LOVE HAS LED YOU TO THIS MOMENT. DO YOU KNOW WHY? BECAUSE MALEBOLGIA'S TOYING WITH YOU-- LETTING YOU BELIEVE YOU'RE STILL HUMAN.
YOU'RE NOT. YOU'RE NECRO-PLASM NOW. AS A CRUEL JOKE, HE LET YOU KEEP SOME-THING.
EVEN THOUGH YOU DON'T NEED IT ANY LONGER.
SO. IT'S TIME TO RELIEVE YOU OF YOUR AGONY.
THE ORIGIN OF ALL YOUR PAIN IS THIS.
YOU'RE CLEANSED NOW, CHILD. MANY IN HELL WILL SMILE THIS NIGHT. IT'S TIME AT LAST FOR YOU TO TAKE THE MANTLE OF THE HELLSPAWN.
GIVE MY REGARDS TO THE OTHER LORDS-- AND THANK YOUR MASTER FOR THE SOUVENIR.

AN INFINITY AWAY, IN THE BLEAKNESS OF HELL'S EIGHTH LEVEL, A KING CACKLES.
HEE HEE HAHAHAHAHA
My warrior's transformation continues as expected. His second incarnation is now complete. With only a bit more modification, Simmons will be ready to take his place in hell's army as a General...
...one devoid of any emotion.
WU BUB
WU BUB
WU BUB
WU BUB

5

MESSIAH

JHROUGH THE CENTURIES IT'S TOUCHED LITERALLY *MILLIONS* OF LIVES-- SOME THROUGH *DIRECT* CONTACT, OTHERS MERELY THE VICTIMS OF FALLOUT THEY WEREN'T EVEN *AWARE* OF. IT'S MERE *EXISTENCE* HAS CAUSED A RIPPLE EFFECT THAT *SWALLOWED* MANY *WORTHY* OF DEATH AND THOUSANDS OF INNOCENTS WHOSE ONLY 'CRIME' WAS TO BE CAUGHT IN ITS *WAKE.*

ITS TIME HAS COME AGAIN. IT IS NOW IN EVIDENCE FOR THE FIRST TIME IN NEARLY *TWO HUNDRED YEARS:*

THE HELLSPAWN. AND THE CURSE HE BRINGS WITH HIM.

AT FIRST, THE CREATURE IS DISORIENTED FROM THE *TRANSFORMATION* AND HAS ONLY LIMITED UNDERSTANDING OF THE *IMPLICATIONS.* AS A RESULT, THE NEW SPAWN WARRIOR THINKS OF THINGS ON A PERSONAL LEVEL EXCLUSIVELY. TRYING *DESPERATELY* TO MAKE SENSE OF HIS RETURN FROM THE GRAVE. IT'S AT THIS TIME THE METAPHORICAL *PEBBLE* HITS THE WATER AND THE OUTWARD RIPPLING BEGINS. HELL *SMILES,* ANTICIPATING THE AVALANCHE OF SOULS TO BE DELIVERED SOON TO THE FLAMING PITS-- GROWING THE *ARMIES* WHICH WILL ONE DAY *OPPOSE HEAVEN.*

THE OFFICER-IN-TRAINING GRASPS NONE OF THIS, AS HE IS CONSUMED BY THE URGE TO REGAIN A LIFE NOW FOREVER LOST.

ALL OF WHICH BRINGS US NOW TO THIS QUIET, NONDESCRIPT HOUSE-- WHICH, AT FIRST GLANCE, APPEARS TO BE JUST LIKE THE *OTHER* HOUSES ON THE BLOCK. AND, IN FACT, IT IS. THOSE WHO *LIVE* WITHIN ITS WALLS ARE WHAT MAKE IT DIFFERENT. ARE WHAT MAKE IT *CURSED.*

FOR THEY HAVE *ALL* BEEN TOUCHED.

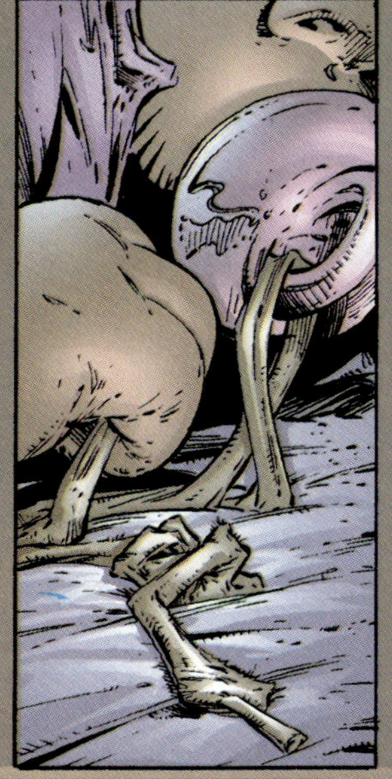

THIS ONE HAS BEEN AT THE **GREATEST** DISTANCE FROM THE CREATURE. SHE HAS HAD BUT A BRIEF ENCOUNTER WITH THE SPAWN WHILE HE WAS IN THE GUISE OF ANOTHER. IT'S HER **MOTHER AND FATHER** WHO'VE BEEN ENMESHED IN THE TRAUMA OF HELL'S NEW WARRIOR.

THAT SITUATION HAS CHANGED.

WHEN SHE FOUND IT AT THE HOSPITAL, SHE FELT THE SAME AS WHEN SHE'S GOTTEN PRESENTS AT CHRISTMAS. WHY? SHE DIDN'T KNOW. IT WAS ONLY A **DIRTY OLD SHOELACE,** BUT SHE FELT COMPELLED TO TURN IT INTO SOME KIND OF **TREASURE.** SO, SHE DUG OUT A **SOOTHER** SHE HADN'T USED IN OVER FOURTEEN MONTHS AND MADE HERSELF A NECKLACE. TONIGHT, SHE WENT BACK TO SUCKING THE SOOTHER, FEELING AN **ATTACHMENT** TO HER NEWFOUND GIFT--

--THE SHOELACE --

--THE UNSUSPECTED **EVIDENCE** THAT **SOMETHING** OR **SOMEONE** HAD INTERVENED AGAINST HER FATHER'S IRREVERSABLE ILLNESS.

JUST DOWN THE HALL RESTS HER MOTHER. SHE WAS ONCE MARRIED TO A MAN NAMED **AL SIMMONS.** HE DIED OVER FIVE YEARS AGO, "IN DEFENSE OF HIS COUNTRY"... OR SO SHE WAS **TOLD.** AT HIS GRAVESITE, THEY GAVE HER AN AMERICAN FLAG AS A TOKEN OF HIS NATION'S GRATITUDE. THOUGH THANKFUL FOR IT, SHE HELD IN HER FIST A MOMENTO OF FAR **GREATER** VALUE:

HER WEDDING BAND.

IT WAS NEARLY A YEAR BEFORE SHE PUT IT ASIDE, AT THE TIME WHEN SHE STARTED DATING ANOTHER MAN, **TERRY FITZGERALD... AL'S BEST FRIEND.** TERRY BROUGHT HAPPINESS INTO HER LIFE. THEY MARRIED ANOTHER YEAR LATER. AND YET, HER FIRST RING STILL SITS NO MORE THAN ARM'S-LENGTH AWAY-- FOREVER KEEPING AL'S MEMORY ALIVE.

SHE IS UNAWARE THAT THE THING CALLED **"SPAWN"** -- THE CREATURE WHO FILLS HER WITH FEAR AND ANXIETY-- IS HER FORMER LOVE, **RETURNED FROM THE DEAD.**

IT'S BEEN OVER THREE HOURS SINCE HE CLOSED HIS EYES, YET THE SLEEP HE SO DESPERATELY WANTS CONTINUES TO EVADE HIM. SINCE HIS "MIRACULOUS" CURE FROM CANCER, REST HASN'T COME EASY. THE DREAMS... OR ARE THEY NIGHTMARES?... CREEP INTO HIS SUBCONSCIOUS, FLASHING RANDOM, SENSELESS IMAGES. FRUSTRATED BY THEIR AMBIGUITY, TERRY LIES THERE IN THE DARK, TRYING TO PIECE THIS PUZZLE TOGETHER.

THE ONLY PHYSICAL CLUE TO HIS RECOVERY -- THE BIZARRE, OVERLOOKED DETAIL -- LIES NOW IN A CRIB, NEXT TO HIS DAUGHTER: THE SHOELACE RIPPED FROM THE VISAGE OF THE HELLSPAWN DURING THE MOMENT OF THAT CREATURE'S UNWILLING, LIFESAVING GESTURE.

TO CURE TERRY. OUT OF LOVE FOR WANDA.

HE'D BEEN WARNED, THE HELLSPAWN HAD, AGAINST USING SUCH A SUDDEN BURST OF ENERGY. GIVEN THE UNSTABLE STATE OF SPAWN'S SYMBIOTIC COSTUME, THE NEXT ABRUPT DRAIN WOULD TRIGGER THE EJECTION OF THE WARRIOR FROM THIS EARTH AND INTO AN EXPEDITION THROUGH HELL.

GREEN NECROPLASMIC ENERGY EXPENDED IN THE CAUSE OF GOOD HAS ONCE AGAIN ADDED TO SPAWN'S MISERY. THE ONLY HOPE REMAINING FOR THE FORMER AL SIMMONS IS AN ETHEREAL CONNECTION TO HIS FRIEND. THOUGH NEITHER IS AWARE OF IT ON ANY LEVEL, THE GREYING AT TERRY'S TEMPLES IS PROOF THE TWO HAD BEEN IN CONTACT...

THAT, AND THE SCRAMBLED IMAGES TRYING TO SPEAK TO TERRY AT NIGHT.

GASP!
IT WOULD BRING HER TOO MUCH PAIN.
NOT REALLY.
GO BACK TO SLEEP. I'M GOING TO GET UP FOR A FEW MINUTES.

JESUS... AL?
HE'S READ THE SIGNAL RIGHT.
IT'S OKAY. YOU'RE HAVING A BAD DREAM, THAT'S ALL.
WANT TO TALK?
WHAT'S WORSE, HE'S NOT READY TO SHARE HIS SUSPICIONS.
THIS IS CRAZY. IT'S BEEN FIVE YEARS. I HELPED BURY HIM, FOR CHRIST'S SAKE.

SOMETHING ISN'T RIGHT. THIS IS THE SECOND TIME SINCE I'VE BEEN HOME FROM THE HOSPITAL THAT IT'S HAPPENED.
WHY?
IS IT SOME SORT IMBALANCE CAUSED BY THE CANCER? THAT'S THE TROUBLE WITH 'MIRACULOUS' RECOVERIES -- NO ONE KNOWS WHAT YOU'RE SUPPOSED TO GO THROUGH AFTERWARDS.
BUT I SWEAR I CAN FEEL HIM -- HIS EMPTINESS.
BEFORE HE'S ABLE TO DRIVE HIMSELF COMPLETELY INSANE, A SERIOUS DOSE OF REALITY THRUSTS ITSELF UPON HIM.
Lick Lick
C'MON, GIRL. EASY NOW! YOUR BREATH ISN'T EXACTLY PERFUME.
SO THE FAMILY PET, ONCE RAISED BY AL SIMMONS HIMSELF, BRINGS A RAY OF LIGHT INTO A POTENTIALLY LONG, DARK NIGHT...
...COMPLETING THE CIRCLE OF FOUR WHO'VE ALL BEEN TOUCHED BY A DEAD MAN.
SINCE REBORN.
FIGHTING TO KEEP HIS SOUL.

THE FIGHT CONTINUES.

ENTERING HELL'S FIFTH LEVEL LIKE SOME DARK, AVENGING ANGEL SHROUDED IN BLOOD BECOMES HIS THIRD TEST. IN THE FIRST TWO HE WAS AN ENEMY.

NOT HERE. NOT NOW.

A ROAR OF PRAISE THUNDERS THROUGH THE SEA OF PEOPLE. EACH NOW BELIEVES THEIR PRAYERS HAVE BEEN ANSWERED.

THEIR SAVIOR IS RETURNED, JUST AS FORETOLD IN SCRIPTURE:

EACH OF US, UPON ENTERING HELL, BECOME PART OF ONE BODY. WE ARE THE UNBELIEVERS. FAITH HAS FLED OUR HEARTS. DESPERATE TO FILL THAT VOID, WE EMBRACED JEALOUSY, LUST AND TREACHERY. OUR ENVY HAS COLORED OUR SKIN, MARKING US NOW AS THE TRUE OUTCASTS. STILL, HOPE HAS NOT ABANDONED US. THERE SHALL COME A DAY WHEN WE WILL BELIEVE AGAIN -- AND HE SHALL BE OUR LIGHT.

DRIPPING BLOOD GAINED IN BATTLE, WE WILL SEE IT IN HIS EYES -- FEEL IT IN HIS HEART. HE HAS MASTERED ENVY.

THE SCRIPTURES ALSO SAID THAT THE RETURNING KING WOULD RULE THROUGH FORCE. 'AN EYE FOR AN EYE' WOULD BECOME LAW.
FOR A TRILLION YEARS, A TRICKLE OF NEW BELIEVERS HAS GROWN TO A MULTITUDE... SO TOO HAS GROWN THEIR IMAGE OF THE SAVIOR.
SPAWN'S ARRIVAL IS GREETED BY A KALEIDOSCOPIC RANGE OF EMOTIONS.
JOY. SKEPTICISM. RAPTURE. ANGER.
SOME BELIEVE. OTHERS DO NOT. THE FIRST TO EXPRESS DOUBT IS QUICKLY 'CONFRONTED.' THOSE WISHING TO ESCAPE HELL'S REACH MUST HAVE FAITH. NONE WILL BE ALLOWED TO CAST ASPERSIONS ON THEIR CHANCE AT HEAVEN.
QUITE PREDICTABLY, THEY FIND AN ANSWER FOR THE QUESTIONER.

THE BLACK LORD CONTROLLED HIS CHILDREN EFFORTLESSLY BY HAVING EACH WAITING FOR A DEITY THAT HE KNEW WOULD NEVER COME.
WHAT ISN'T PREDICTABLE IS SPAWN BEING THERE IN THE FIRST PLACE.
THE PROPHECIES OF SCRIPTURE WERE NEVER SUPPOSED TO COME TO PASS. THEY WERE LIES-- FABRICATIONS OF THE DEVIL WHO RULES UNSEEN OVER THE FIFTH LEVEL.
EACH INDIVIDUAL'S PUNISHMENT WAS TO PRAY AN ETERNITY FOR SALVATION. A FAITH IN THE PROMISES OF SCRIPTURE WAS ALL THEY HAD LEFT.
GET THE HELL OFF ME!!!
THOSE WANTING TO WORSHIP HIM AND THOSE READY TO FLAY HIM STUMBLE OVER EACH OTHER TRYING TO REACH SPAWN FIRST.
THE CLOAKED HERO CARES FOR NEITHER.

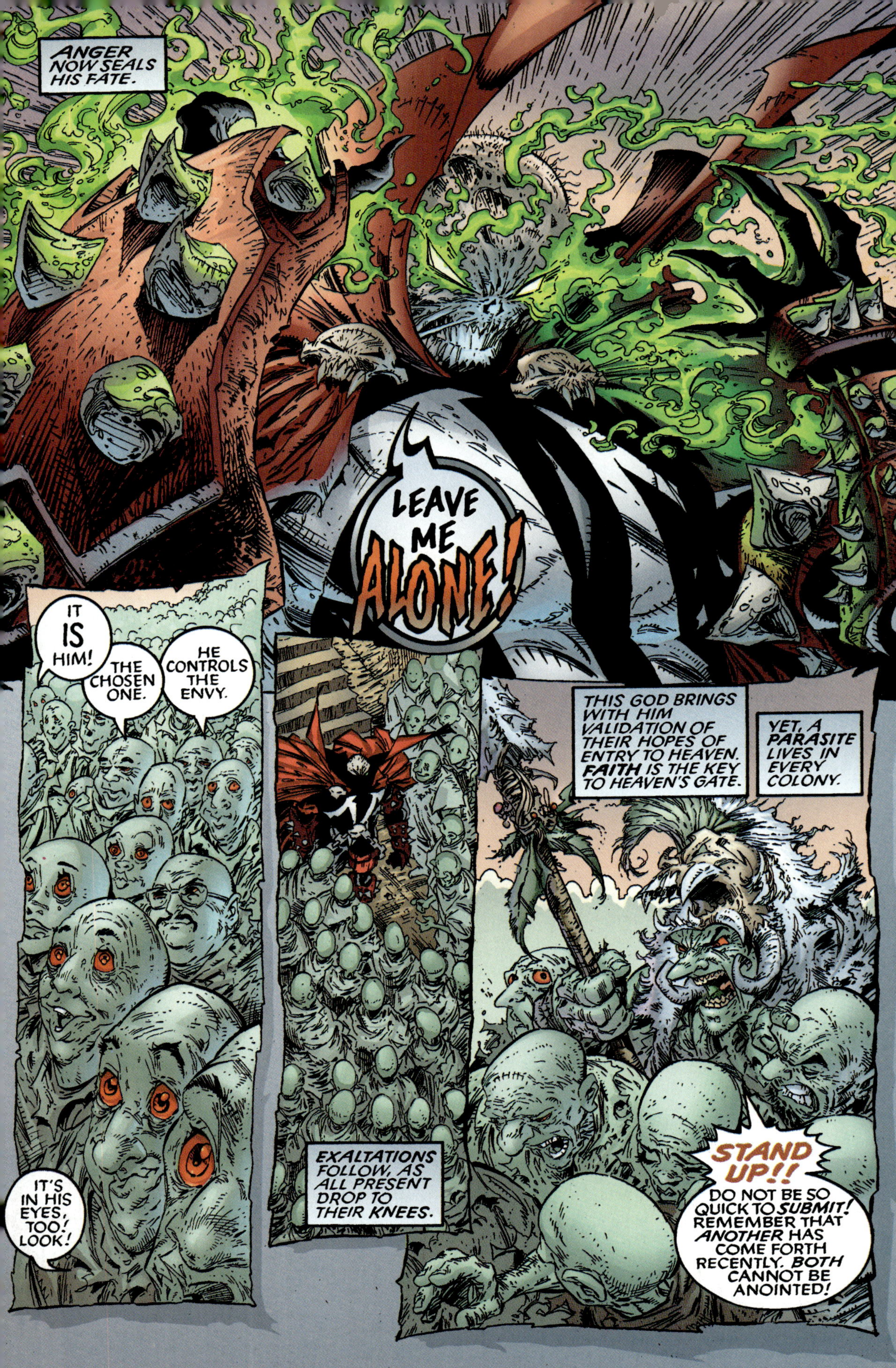

ANGER NOW SEALS HIS FATE.
LEAVE ME ALONE!
IT IS HIM!
THE CHOSEN ONE.
HE CONTROLS THE ENVY.
IT'S IN HIS EYES, TOO! LOOK!
EXALTATIONS FOLLOW, AS ALL PRESENT DROP TO THEIR KNEES.
THIS GOD BRINGS WITH HIM VALIDATION OF THEIR HOPES OF ENTRY TO HEAVEN. FAITH IS THE KEY TO HEAVEN'S GATE.
YET, A PARASITE LIVES IN EVERY COLONY.
STAND UP!!
DO NOT BE SO QUICK TO SUBMIT! REMEMBER THAT ANOTHER HAS COME FORTH RECENTLY. BOTH CANNOT BE ANOINTED!

WE'VE WAITED AN INFINITY FOR THIS DAY-- HOPING, PRAYING FOR OUR SALVATION. BUT NOW WE'VE GOTTEN TWO SIGNALS IN LESS THAN A DAY.
I CAN'T.
HOW DO WE KNOW YOU CAN SAVE US?
MODESTY. ANOTHER SIGN OF THE MESSIAH.

WHAT DO YOU MEAN, YOU CAN'T? THEN WHY ARE YOU HERE NOW?

AFTER A MOMENT'S HESITATION, SPAWN GIVES THE SHORT VERSION.
BECAUSE I LOVED MY WIFE.
SO THEY KILLED ME.

IT BEGINS.
THOSE CLOSEST TO THE CONVERSATION REPEAT WHAT THEY'VE JUST HEARD.

AS IT SPREADS FAR AND WIDE THROUGH THE CROWD, IT BECOMES THE GOSPEL.

BY THE TIME IT'S HALF-WAY THROUGH THE CROWD, IT'S TAKEN ON A LIFE OF ITS OWN.

HE KILLED HIS WIFE AND LOVED. IT.

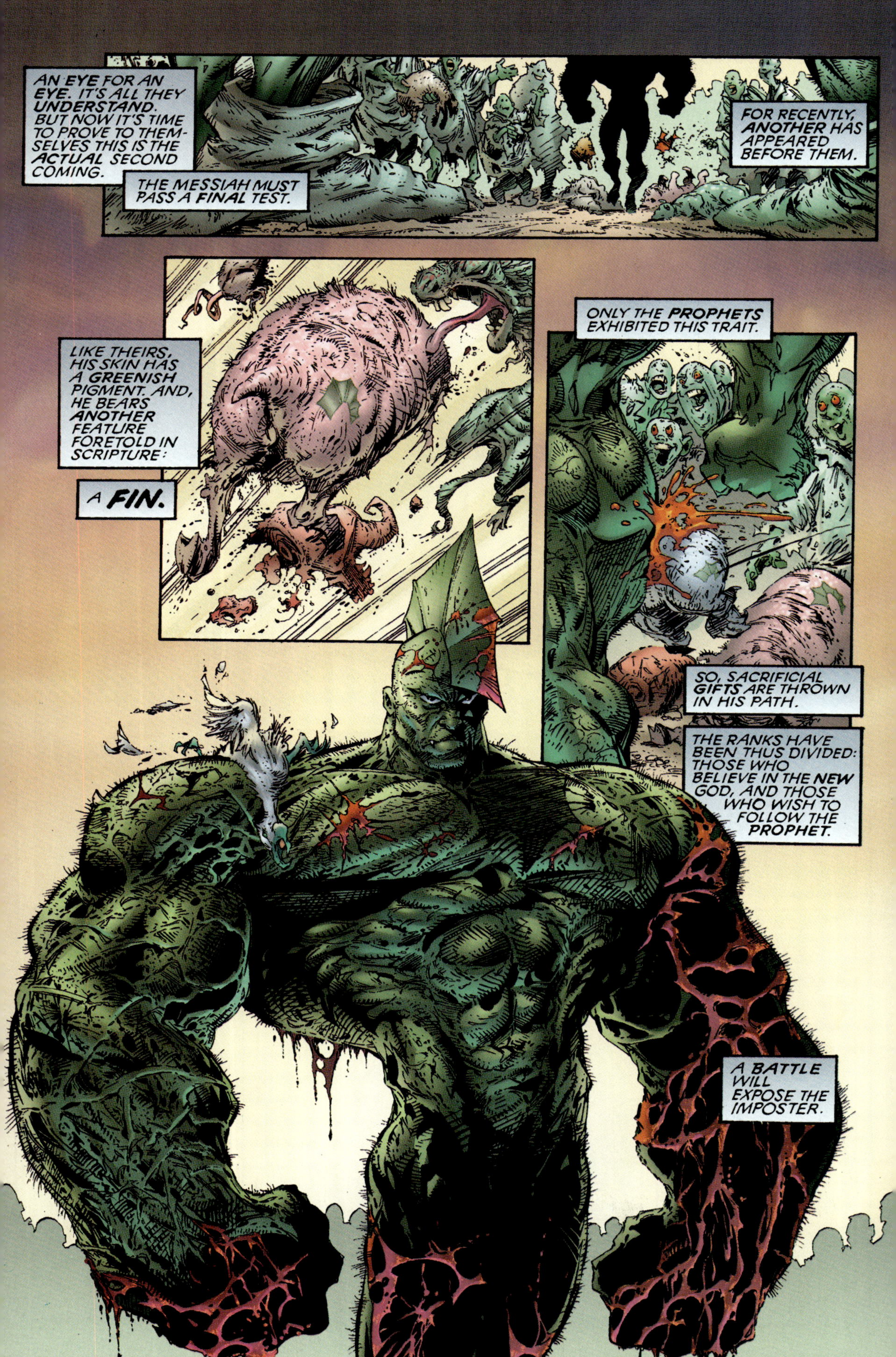

AN EYE FOR AN EYE. IT'S ALL THEY UNDERSTAND. BUT NOW IT'S TIME TO PROVE TO THEM- SELVES THIS IS THE ACTUAL SECOND COMING.
THE MESSIAH MUST PASS A FINAL TEST.
FOR RECENTLY, ANOTHER HAS APPEARED BEFORE THEM.
LIKE THEIRS, HIS SKIN HAS A GREENISH PIGMENT. AND, HE BEARS ANOTHER FEATURE FORETOLD IN SCRIPTURE:
A FIN.
ONLY THE PROPHETS EXHIBITED THIS TRAIT.
SO, SACRIFICIAL GIFTS ARE THROWN IN HIS PATH.
THE RANKS HAVE BEEN THUS DIVIDED: THOSE WHO BELIEVE IN THE NEW GOD, AND THOSE WHO WISH TO FOLLOW THE PROPHET.
A BATTLE WILL EXPOSE THE IMPOSTER.

LET'S GET THIS OVER WITH.
SPAWN STARES INTENTLY FOR A MOMENT, TRYING TO PLACE HIS NEW FOE, WITHOUT SUCCESS.
HE TELLS HIMSELF IT'S JUST ANOTHER STRANGER TRYING TO BLUR HIS EXISTENCE.
ANOTHER OBSTACLE.
HELL HAS BECOME NO DIFFERENT FROM EARTH.
ALWAYS ON THE ATTACK, OR TAKING THINGS.
NEVER GIVING BACK.

WHAT'S WORSE IS THAT SPAWN CHOSE TO RETURN TO THE PITS OF HELL. HE SACRIFICED HIMSELF TO KEEP A WIFE WHO FEARS HIM HAPPY. *
*ISSUE 50.--Tom.
AFTER ALL, HOW CAN A DEAD, CURSED SOUL IN HELL MAKE HIS SITUATION ANY WORSE?
HIS VICIOUS, RAGING ATTACK KNOWS NO BOUNDS.
INNOCENTS ARE CAUGHT IN THE FRAY.
ON EARTH, HIS USE OF HIS POWERS HAD TO BE DISCREET. IN HIS CURRENT STATE OF DAMNATION, HOW-EVER, A BERSERKER'S BELIGERANCE IS CON-SIDERED A VIRTUE.
HE DOESN'T RELENT UNTIL HIS GOAL IS MET:
ABSOLUTE VICTORY OVER HIS GREEN FOE.

HIS OPPONENT DRAWS A DEEP BREATH.

THE NEXT SOUND TO LEAVE HIS MOUTH IS LOST IN THE DIN OF A THOUSAND FOOTFALLS:

hee hee

BLASPHEMER
DEFILER
FALSE PROPHET
DIE
DIE
DIE

RAGE BOILS OVER. THEY'LL NOT ENDURE SUCH DIS-RESPECT TOWARD THEIR DAMNATION.

THEIR ETERNAL WAIT HAS EARNED THEM AT LEAST THAT COMPENSATION.

EVEN IF THE TRES-PASSER DOES BEAR 'THE MARK'.

AND AS THE HULKING FIGURE IS MARCHED AWAY LIKE SOME HUNTER'S PRIZE KILL, HIS REACTION IS EVEN MORE STARTLING.

SPAWN SWEARS HE HEARS SOME-THING THAT JUST CAN'T BE:

GIGGLING.

A GLORIOUS CELEBRATION ENSUES, ENGULFING MOST OF THE GATHERING. THEIR KING HAS FINALLY COME FOR THEM. ALL SHALL BE SAVED.
WITH ONE EXCEPTION.
SO WHAT HAPPENS TO HIM?
WHEN THE DARKNESS COMES, HE'LL DIE.
WHEN HE APPEARED, HE GAVE US HOPE. HIS DEFEAT SHOWS HOW WE WERE BETRAYED, MY LORD.
SO HE IS BEING PREPARED-- BEFOULED WITH GRIME, FED HIS LAST MEAL, THEN SHOWERED IN URINE.
HIS CROSS IS BEING READIED. THE STONING WILL TAKE BUT A FEW MINUTES.
CRIMES AGAINST THE FAITH WILL NOT BE PERMITTED. ESPECIALLY THOSE COMMITTED BY HIS KIND.
I'D LIKE TO SPEAK TO HIM... ...PRIVATELY.
OF COURSE, MY LORD.

WHAT NOW? COME HERE TO DO A LITTLE GLOATING?

NOPE. I DON'T HAVE TO. YOU ALREADY KNOW WHAT I CAN DO.

STILL, I'M CURIOUS ABOUT SOMETHING. OUT OF ALL YOUR PEOPLE, WHY WERE YOU SELECTED TO TAKE ME ON?

THOSE AREN'T "MY" PEOPLE. LOOK... YOU WANT TO FIGURE THIS OUT, GREAT. TO ME, THIS IS ALL SOME SCREWY DREAM OR HALLUCINATION.

BUT IF IT'LL MAKE YOU FEEL ANY BETTER, I'LL SPILL MY GUTS. SEE, I'M FROM CHICAGO, SOME BIG CITY IN AMERICA. MY JOB IS TRYING TO CLEAN IT UP, WHICH MEANS I DEAL WITH PSYCHOS EVERY DAY. THE LAST ONE WAS SOME BROAD WHO CALLS HERSELF THE FIEND. * DON'T ASK ME WHY, BUT FOR SOME REASON SHE'S GOT THIS HARD-ON TO WIPE ME OUT. SO WE MET, AND SHE BLEW OFF MY ARMS.

AND THAT'S THE LAST I RECALL OF REALITY.

MY GUESS IS, SHE SHOT ME FULL OF DRUGS AND I'M TRIPPING OUT RIGHT NOW--

-- BECAUSE NEXT THING I KNOW I APPEAR IN HELL, BUCK NAKED, WITH BOTH ARMS BACK. AND EVERYONE I MEET THINKS I'M SOME GODDAMN PROPHET. MY FIN MEANS SOMETHING SPIRITUAL TO THEM.

WHEN YOU SHOWED UP, I WAS REDUCED TO SECOND BANANA. WHO WANTS A PROPHET WHEN A GOD COMES CALLING?

BESIDES, IT REALLY PISSED THEM OFF WHEN I SAID THEIR MESSIAH WOULDN'T APPEAR FOR ANOTHER FORTY THOUSAND YEARS.

AND THAT JUSTIFIES KILLING YOU?

LIKE I SAID, THIS IS JUST SOME NIGHTMARE. THEY WANTED A FIGHT, I GAVE IT TO THEM. ONE OF US HAD TO FAIL.

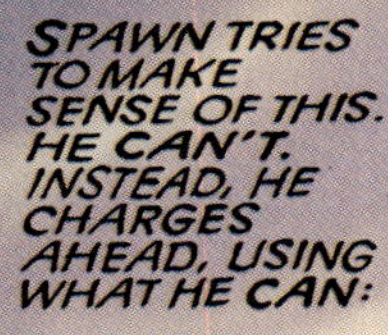

SPAWN TRIES TO MAKE SENSE OF THIS. HE CAN'T. INSTEAD, HE CHARGES AHEAD, USING WHAT HE CAN:

THEIR BLIND FAITH.

IF THEY WANT A MESSIAH, SO BE IT.

LIKE A STAMPEDE OF CATTLE, THE MOB CRUSHES SPAWN UNDER ITS SHEER WEIGHT.
RAVENOUS FOR BLOOD.
NEVER WOULD THE HOLY LEADER SUCH A DEMEANING ORDER AS, "FORGIVE."
"AN EYE FOR AN EYE."
SO IT IS WRITTEN. SO IT SHALL BE.
LEGEND HAS SPOKEN OF THIS ENEMY ALSO. HOW THE FALSE GOD BEARS A SYMBOL OF HIS VILENESS.
A CALL TO 'TURN THE OTHER CHEEK' COMES ONLY FROM THE GREATEST SINNER.
SPAWN DIDN'T HAVE ONE. THAT DIDN'T MATTER. HE DID NOW.
THE CARVING WAS CRUDE.

YOUR RECKONING IS AT HAND.
THEY WILL SOON KNOW IN THE OTHER LEVELS NOT TO TRIFLE WITH OUR PRAYERS. YOUR DEATHS SHALL BE A TRIUMPHAL TESTAMENT TO OUR FAITH--

-- REDEDICATING US TO OUR COMING SALVATION.
YOU BOTH SHALL DIE, FOREVER MARKED AS TRAITORS. DESPITE YOU, WE SHALL OVERCOME.
THE SELF-IMPOSED LEADER TURNS TO HIS MASSES.
LET HE WHO IS WITH SIN CAST THE FIRST STONE!
SADLY FOR THEM, THEIR WEAPONS WILL NOT STRIKE THEIR INTENDED TARGETS.
THE CRUCIFIED PAIR VANISH IN A BLINK.

THEIR VENGEANCE NOW DENIED, THE OCCUPANTS OF HELL'S FIFTH LEVEL CAN ONLY RETURN TO THEIR BELOVED ALTAR. IT IS, AFTER ALL, THE EXACT SPOT WHERE THE TRUE GOD WILL RETURN. SO IT IS WRITTEN. SO IT SHALL BE.

BUT NONE WILL BE ABLE TO PREDICT THEIR ACTUAL FUTURE: THAT OF ABJECT DAMNATION. IN THEIR FAITH HAS NOW BEEN PLANTED A SEED OF DOUBT, AND IN THAT ENVIRONMENT THESE ACRES OF GREEN SOULS WILL DECLINE INTO ROT.

EACH BELIEVES THEIRS IS THE TRUE PATH TO CLEANSING. ANY DISAGREEMENTS WILL AT FIRST BE PEACEFUL-- PHILOSOPHICAL -- THEN ESCALATE WITH CHILLING EASE INTO BATTLE LINES DRAWN BETWEEN ENEMIES.

ANARCHY WILL BE THE RULE, SET IN MOTION FOR THE NEXT MILLION YEARS BY A PUPPET USED IN AN UNHOLY WAR.

THE ARRIVAL OF THIS SPAWN, NOW BRANDED, HAS SET FOREVER IN MOTION THESE CATA-CLYSMIC EVENTS. HIS LORD, THE EVIL MALEBOLGIA, HAS FINALLY FOUND A WAY TO EVEN A PERSONAL SCORE WITH THE RULER OF LEVEL FIVE.

FOR, THOUGH HELL DOES SEEK TO CONQUER THE POWERS OF GOOD, ITS LORDS ALSO SEEK TO EVISCERATE EACH OTHER.

IMAGINE WHAT THESE HELLISH BEINGS WOULD LEAVE IN THEIR WAKE ON THIS EARTH...!

NEXT:
SPAWN VS. MALEBOLGIA

6

The ABYSS. A HARSH BLACKNESS SO DENSE NO *LIGHT* HAS EVER INTRUDED HERE. WHILE GOD WAS CREATING THE COSMOS, GIVING LIFE TO EVERY CORNER, HIS OMNISCIENT PRESENCE CAST A *SHADOW*. PLANTED THERE AS WELL WAS A SEED. IT GREW STEADILY IN THE COLD PALL OF THE ALMIGHTY.

THIS PATCH OF INFINITY, JUST TO THE LEFT OF THE PRECIOUS LIGHT, IS NOW A *HARVEST GROUND* FOR THE DIVINELY THWARTED SEED.

SEED WE NOW CALL *SIN*.

IT GERMINATES IN MEN OF *WEAKNESS*. LUST, GREED, AND THE OTHER DEADLY SINS TAKE ROOT IN THEM.

EMBEDDED NOW IN THIS DARK LOAM IS A MAN CONDEMNED BY HIS OWN ACTS UPON HUMANITY:

Lt. COLONEL AL SIMMONS.

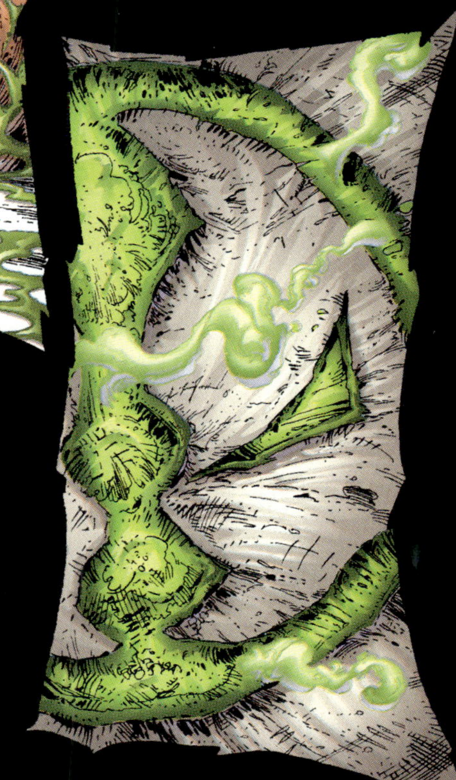

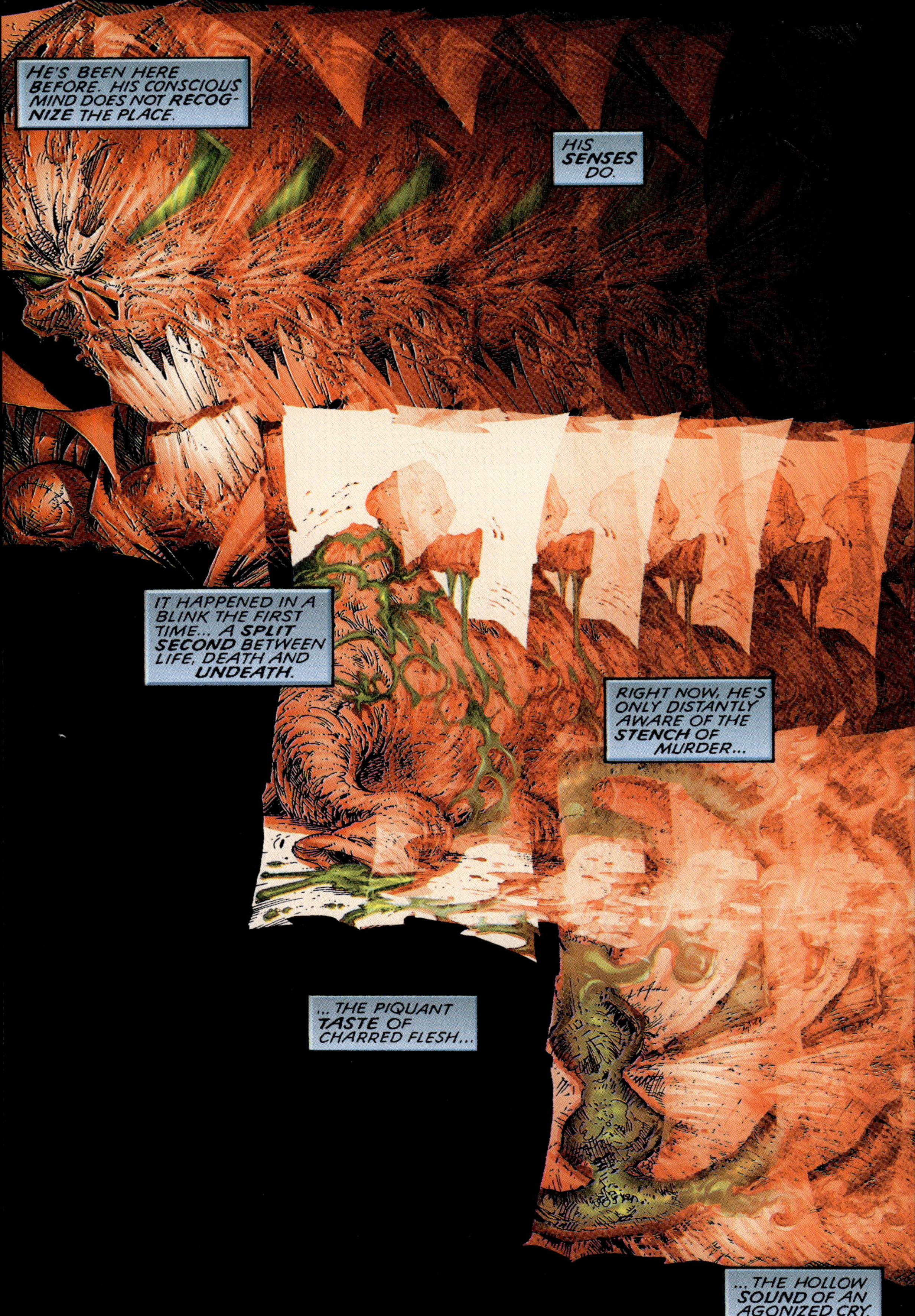

HE'S BEEN HERE BEFORE. HIS CONSCIOUS MIND DOES NOT RECOGNIZE THE PLACE.
HIS SENSES DO.
IT HAPPENED IN A BLINK THE FIRST TIME... A SPLIT SECOND BETWEEN LIFE, DEATH AND UNDEATH.
RIGHT NOW, HE'S ONLY DISTANTLY AWARE OF THE STENCH OF MURDER...
...THE PIQUANT TASTE OF CHARRED FLESH...
...THE HOLLOW SOUND OF AN AGONIZED CRY.

IT'S ALL SO FAMILIAR.
WHERE HE WAS CURSED.
THIS IS WHERE HE DIED.
IN EXCHANGE FOR THAT UNHOLY BLESSING HE PAID THE ULTIMATE PRICE: HE RELENQUISHED HIS SHARE OF ETERNITY.
HE IS RETURNED NOW TO HIS DEMONIC BIRTHPLACE.
WHERE HE MADE HIS DEAL.

NO.

LEVEL NINE.

THE NIGHTMARISH REALM THAT VOMITED SPAWN BACK TO LIFE.

WHOSE RULER CRAVES THAT WHICH HE HIMSELF WAS NOT FURNISHED: SOULS.

THEY ARE EITHER GIVEN OVER AT DEATH OR SURRENDERED WILLINGLY BY THOSE WHO REJECT GOD. EACH SOUL HELPS TO AMASS AN ARMY FIT TO CONQUER THE HEAVENS.

LORDING OVER IT ALL IS THE DEVIL KNOWN AS THE MALEBOLGIA. HE WAITS OUT THE SLOW CENTURIES UNTIL THE BATTLE WITH GOD IS DECLARED...

...UNTIL HIS ARMY WILL VANQUISH THE LIGHT.

INTO EVERY CORNER, THE SHADOWS WILL SEEP--

--DRIVING HOME THE VICTORY HIS GENERALS HAVE WON.

AL SIMMONS IS EXPECTED TO ONE DAY BECOME SUCH A GENERAL...
...WHICH IS WHY SPAWN IS NOW BEING PUT THROUGH THE PACES. MALEBOLGIA WISHES TO SEE HIS POTENTIAL FIRST-HAND...
...TO BEST GAUGE WHETHER HE'LL BE ABLE TO GERMINATE THE EVIL LIVING DEEP WITHIN SIMMONS' BEING.
UMPFF
SO THERE MUST BE TESTS.
MIXED WITH CRUEL IRONY.
KINCAID!
you scream, i scream. we both scream for ice cream
HE'D KILLED HIM ONCE BEFORE, SPAWN HAD. *
*ISSUE 5 -- Tom-

BUT THIS IS HELL. THIS IS NOW.
LOGIC ISN'T ACCORDED ANY FAVORS. INSTINCTIVELY, SPAWN KNOWS THIS. MORE IMPORTANTLY, HE ACCEPTS IT WITHOUT QUESTION.
ON EARTH, BILLY KINCAID HAD FALLEN TO THE LOWEST POSSIBLE LEVEL KNOWN TO MAN: A MURDERING PEDOPHILE.
STRIPPING CHILDREN OF THEIR INNOCENCE... AND SOCIETY OF ITS CHILDREN.
THE HELLSPAWN DISEMBOWELS HIM A SECOND TIME WHILE WISHING THAT KINCAID WILL TRY TO GET UP SO HE CAN GUT HIM AGAIN.
AND SO, SPAWN HAS PASSED THIS TEST.

HE DESERVED IT. THANK YOU, AL.
WANDA!!!?
I KNOW WHAT YOU'RE THINKING, BUT IT REALLY IS ME, SWEETHEART.
GOD, HOW CAN THIS BE?!
BECAUSE I WANTED IT. TO BE BY YOUR SIDE... FOREVER. I KNOW THAT GOD SCORNS THOSE WHO TAKE THEIR OWN LIVES...
...BUT SUICIDE WAS THE ONLY CHOICE. WE HAVE TO BE TOGETHER.
HE STARES IN HER EYES. THEY DON'T LIE.
HE CHERISHES THIS ELUSIVE MOMENT AS THEY EMBRACE.
THE WAIT HAS BEEN SO VERY LONG.
I DIDN'T MEAN FOR ANY OF THIS TO HAPPEN.

I KNOW YOU DIDN'T, AL. BUT I'M HERE... WE'RE HERE. ALL OF US.
YOU WERE ALWAYS TOO MUCH MAN FOR ONE WOMAN.
NOW YOU CAN HAVE ME ANY WAY YOU WANT. FAITHFUL. LUSTFUL. ADORING.
IT DOESN'T MATTER WHAT EMOTION YOU FEEL. WE... I CAN FULFILL YOU. "TILL DEATH DO US PART." REMEMBER THAT, OUR WEDDING VOW?
IT DOESN'T HAVE TO END. WE CAN SATISFY ALL YOUR DESIRES.
FOR ONE BRIEF, FROZEN MOMENT, AL SIMMONS BELIEVES HIS TORMENT IS FINALLY AT AN END. EUPHORIA REIGNS. HIS CURSE HAS BEEN LIFTED.

A TEST.
AS HE FALLS, IT STILL DOESN'T REGISTER. THIS IS A HOAX. A SHAM.
EXPLOITING THE WEAKNESS THAT FOREVER DAMNED HIM: HIS LOVE FOR HIS BEAUTIFUL WIFE.
SHE'S THE REASON HE NOW EXISTS, WHY HE HAD TO GO ON IN THIS NEW, WRETCHED FORM.
HE CLOSES HIS EYES AS SHE POUNCES...
HE WON'T LET THAT HAPPEN.
BUT NOW THEY'RE MOCKING HER AND WHAT SHE REPRESENTS.
...NOT WANTING TO WITNESS WHAT MUST NOW BE DONE.

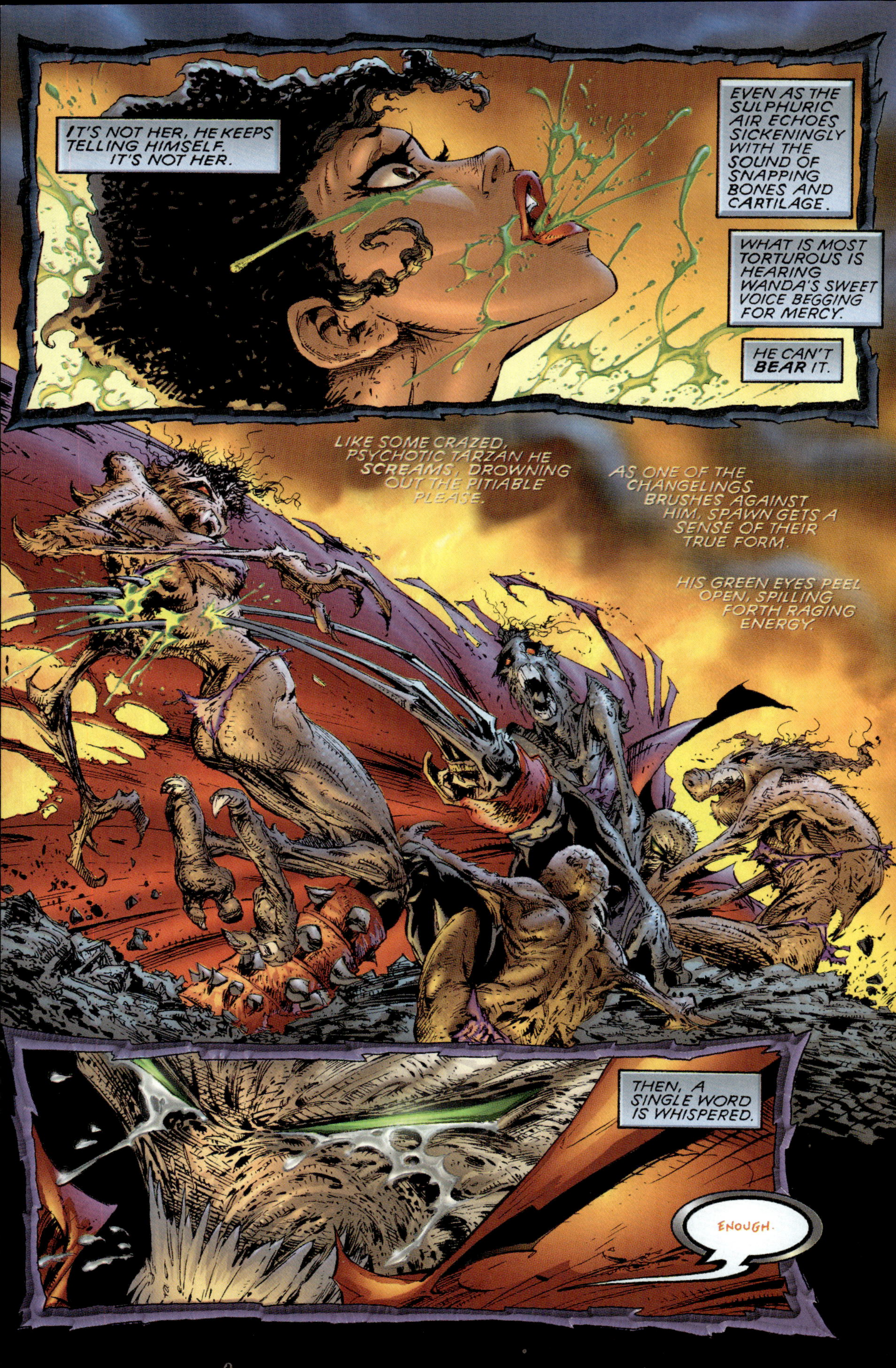

IT'S NOT HER, HE KEEPS TELLING HIMSELF. IT'S NOT HER.
EVEN AS THE SULPHURIC AIR ECHOES SICKENINGLY WITH THE SOUND OF SNAPPING BONES AND CARTILAGE.
WHAT IS MOST TORTUROUS IS HEARING WANDA'S SWEET VOICE BEGGING FOR MERCY.
HE CAN'T BEAR IT.
LIKE SOME CRAZED, PSYCHOTIC TARZAN HE SCREAMS, DROWNING OUT THE PITIABLE PLEASE.
AS ONE OF THE CHANGELINGS BRUSHES AGAINST HIM, SPAWN GETS A SENSE OF THEIR TRUE FORM.
HIS GREEN EYES PEEL OPEN, SPILLING FORTH RAGING ENERGY.
THEN, A SINGLE WORD IS WHISPERED.
ENOUGH.

GODDAMMIT, I'VE SUFFERED ENOUGH!
MALEBOLGIA WANTS A WAR. HE'S GOT IT! I DON'T GIVE A CRAP ANYMORE.
SEND YOUR PUPPETS! EVERY LAST ONE OF THEM. I'LL TAKE 'EM.
YOU WANT ME TO BE LIKE YOU, FINE. I'LL BE VICIOUS, EVIL, SOULLESS!! AFTER I'VE RIPPED YOUR THROAT OUT.
YOU BASTARD. THIS IS GOING TO END.

A PATH OF SLAUGHTERED DEMONS TRAILS UP THE DARK MOUNTAINSIDE. HOW LONG IT TOOK HIM, HE DOESN'T CARE. HE'S WHERE HE WANTS TO BE AND NOTHING WAS ABLE TO PREVENT THAT.
THE BLOOD-CLOAKED WARRIOR HAS WON, PASSING YET ANOTHER TEST.
NOW IT'S YOUR TURN, DEVIL!
CREATION MEETS CREATOR. THIS OFFICIALLY SETS THE SCENE.
Contain your petty threats, Simmons. Ignorance does not befit your stature. You see, my child, though you were impressive in that little skirmish, you still grasp only a fraction of the truth about yourself.
I DON'T CARE!
Then do something about it.
BELIEVE ME, I INTEND TO.

'CAUSE YOU DON'T SCARE ME. KNOW WHY? THERE'S NOTHING LEFT FOR YOU TO TAKE. I'M EMPTY. DRAINED.
BUT I'LL NEVER BE YOUR SLAVE.
NEVER!
SUDDENLY, THE GROUND SHIFTS--
--AS A SICKLY CACKLE REVERBERATES THROUGH THE CORRIDORS OF HELL.
HAHAHAHA
Don't delude yourself, Simmons. It's far too late for you to attain inner peace.

You don't even know what you're fighting against, or why. How can you even hope to slay me when I'm not there...
..I'm here.
Or am I?
Machines like you are very rare--built with just the right wiring. You could have been an instrument of God's elite. Instead, you pimped yourself--
--allowing others to trigger your senses. Manipulate your logic--

You're off-balance, Simmons... exactly where I want you to be: questioning your own sanity. What's this all about?
Well, let me enlighten you...
Just like this version of Hell that surrounds you.
--just like I did. It's not about good or evil. Those are concepts created by man. Very limited.

It appears as your subconscious believes it should. You humans have such narrow imaginations.

Sin. Evil. Terror. They wear many forms. So do their masters.

Shadows were created in Hell. Their tendrils encroach on God's light, and creep through to Earth.

How can you possibly kill that which is everywhere at once?

I live in all you see. In all shapes.

And, to the place that welcomes me most of all: the heart of man.

From the lowly insects.

To the beasts.

That's how I got you. Because your heart wanted me. Needed me. All that you've become has always been your choice.
You became a trained killer willingly, and I watched as you grew more and more efficient at it.
THEN TAKE ME. MY SOUL, WHATEVER THE HELL YOU WANT--
--JUST LEAVE MY WIFE ALONE. SHE'S NOT A PART OF THIS.
Unfortunately, she is.
And as for your soul, it's already mine... so you've nothing left to barter.
YES, I DO.
MY LOYALTY.
YOU DON'T CONTROL THAT. I'VE TAKEN YOUR POWERS, YOUR COSTUME, AND WHATEVER IT IS I'VE BECOME, BUT YOU STILL DON'T CONTROL ME.

YOU JUST OWN ME. THAT'S ALL. MY MIND'S STILL FREE, AND I REJECT ALL OF THIS. YOU'VE FAILED, MALEBOLGIA.
GOD'S LAUGHING AT YOU.
Listen here, worm! You're nothing! You were only reborn because I wanted it. Because I let you come back.
So, fine. Convince yourself that you're free. Play whatever mind games you need to. Because, believe me, I do control you.
Your emotions are mine. They're what Jason Wynn manipulated. He ordered you to commit atrocitities. You gave in.
If anyone should be laughing it's me, right in God's face. He lost His grip on one of His potential elite. And one day, you and he shall face each other as enemies.

That will lead to my victory.
You are becoming exactly what I intended. Your rage. Instincts. They're perfect. Your half-hearted rejection of these circumstances, all part of the process. To become my Grim Reaper. My messenger.
I've even given you a few more tools.*
The Visage of death.
The Black Heart of death.
And the Mark.
*THE LAST THREE ISSUES --Tom.

Slowly, I've made you over, in my image--
--transforming you into one of my greatest warriors. So, where there was failure we now find grandeur. Death now takes relentless strides. Return, my Hellspawn, to your beginnings.
The Earth needs you-- for, without an agent of Death, souls cannot be harvested.
And my army must grow.
As with your loyalty, I need your servitude. In time, that will come.
Let that time be now.
Be my executor. Work for me and I promise to leave your wife untouched.
Pure.

"Now go. Stimulate corruption in your wake. Enter the minds of men. Disrupt their dreams and spread my gospel."
EARTH. 2:54 A.M.
TERRY. I'M HERE.
WHO ARE YOU? TELL ME!
YOU ALREADY KNOW.
WHAT DO YOU MEAN?
LOOK AT ME. INTO MY EYES.
WHAT DO YOU SEE?

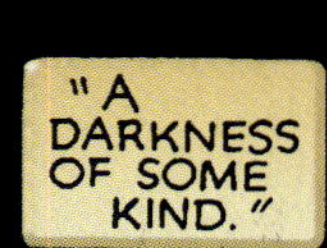
"A DARKNESS OF SOME KIND."
NO!

YOU SEE ME. YOUR FRIEND.

LOOK AGAIN.
"MY GOD. IT'S TRUE."

YOU'RE BACK! ALIVE!
AL!
...YOU'RE ALIVE...
TERRY FITZGERALD WILL SIT THERE, SHAKING, UNTIL THE SHADOWS WITHDRAW FROM DAWN'S LIGHT.

"HELTER SKELTER"

Todd McFarlane – *story*
Greg Capullo – *pencils*
Danny Miki – *inks*
Tom Orzechowski – *copy editor & letters*
Brian Haberlin & Dan Kemp – *colour*

"CHOICES" PART ONE

Todd McFarlane – *story & art*
Danny Miki – *inks*
Tom Orzechowski – *copy editor & letters*
Brian Haberlin, Dan Kemp &
Todd Broeker – *colour*

"CHOICES" PART TWO

Todd McFarlane – *story*
Greg Capullo – *pencils*
Danny Miki – *inks*
Tom Orzechowski – *copy editor & letters*
Brian Haberlin, Dan Kemp &
Todd Broeker – *colour*

"FREEFALL"

Todd McFarlane – *story & inks*
Greg Capullo – *pencils*
Danny Miki – *inks*
Tom Orzechowski – *copy editor & letters*
Brian Haberlin & Dan Kemp – *colour*

"MESSIAH"

Todd McFarlane – *story & inks*
Greg Capullo – *pencils*
Danny Miki – *inks*
Tom Orzechowski – *copy editor & letters*
Brian Haberlin, Dan Kemp & Matt Milla – *colour*

"THE RECKONING"

Todd McFarlane – *story & inks*
Greg Capullo – *pencils*
Danny Miki – *inks*
Tom Orzechowski – *copy editor & letters*
Brian Haberlin & Dan Kemp – *colour*

S P A W N ®
C O L L E C T I O N S   F R O M
T I T A N   B O O K S

N O W   A V A I L A B L E . . .

SPAWN®: SANCTION
ISBN 1 84023 019 3

A new warrior angel emerges to challenge Spawn, and Tremor returns.
To order telephone 01858 433169.

Copyright © 1996 Todd McFarlane Productions, Inc. All rights reserved.

S P A W N ®
C O L L E C T I O N S   F R O M
T I T A N   B O O K S

C O M I N G   S O O N . . .

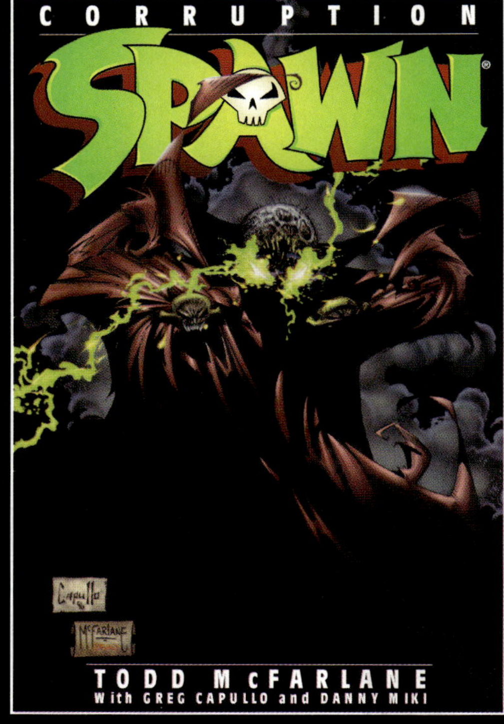

SPAWN®: CORRUPTION
ISBN 1 84023 031 2

Spawn submits to the will of Malebolgia, and forms a new alliance with
an old friend.
To order telephone 01858 433169.

Copyright © 1996, 1997 Todd McFarlane Productions, Inc. All rights reserved.